ONE SECOND AFTER ANOTHER

THE AFTER ANOTHER TRILOGY, BOOK 3

BETHANY-KRIS

Published by Bethany-Kris

www.bethanykris.com

ISBN 13: 978-1-989658-34-5

Editor: Elizabeth Peters

Cover Design © London Miller

National Sexual Assault Hotline: 800.656.HOPE (4673)
Chat Online: online.rainn.org

CONTENTS

1.

Present Day, Nevada …

MERE seconds could change everything. Even, the span of time it took Luca to open his eyes and know he was alone in the hotel room. He didn't need to turn in the bed to see it was empty of Penny's presence. He felt the loss.

Knew it was *real* before it actually was. The weight sitting on his chest, and the cold cloud surrounding him made the white ceiling seem like it was closing down in on him. The absolute silence—but for his steady breaths and the beats of his heart—confirmed what he already knew even though he didn't want to believe it.

He was alone.

Absolutely.

"Penny," he dared to call.

Daring himself to be wrong.

Willing her to prove him wrong, even.

His call went unanswered.

Before that moment, Luca hadn't realized loneliness could be such a tangible thing. Beyond a feeling, there was a real presence about it. A heaviness around him that made it all the more real.

And cruel.

There was something to be said about the way loneliness could leave a man confused. Like as he sat up in the bed, confirming Penny's side was empty and so was the rest of the room, he just couldn't catch up to speed. He was quite aware Penny wasn't beside him in the bed like she had been the night before when they fell asleep. And yet, a part of him didn't want to believe that even when he grabbed the blanket and yanked it away from her empty pillow. Even the indentation of her head was gone.

The room was just … chilly.

When had she gotten up?

Did she leave or—

"Penny!"

Luca's shout undoubtedly carried out through the bedroom door to the rest of the hotel room, but to no avail. He didn't get an answer just like the first time.

Fuck.

He was trying not to panic. Excuses raced through his mind in a shitty attempt to quell how the nervousness skimming over his skin when he exited the bed. Cold floors met the soles of his feet while he thought … *she's just getting food—maybe coffee.* Shit, he couldn't pretend to know what Penny did during her days. He'd only been back in her life for a short while. Who was to say she didn't have an entire routine in the mornings, right?

Bullshit.

He knew it.

His heart screamed it.

Of course, that didn't stop his sleepy brain from trying to brush off the *obvious.* Like the differences in the bedroom—the shoes Penny had kicked to the side were now gone. Her laptop sat open on the chair, but only the back of the screen faced him. As if she had been sitting there with it, and just left it where it was because she wouldn't need it. The wall safe next to the bed had been left open.

Why didn't he hear that?

Right.

Because he thought he was safe. Stupidly, he believed that he had the upper hand where Penny was concerned. Why would she leave again? Hell, she brought *him* here.

That's why it didn't make sense. Why he couldn't catch up, so to speak.

The obvious stared him in the face as he gathered his clothes from the night before in his arms and headed for the connected bathroom, but he still refused to accept it. He had one leg stuffed into the pair of jeans and was shoving in his second leg as he came to a complete stop in the doorway of the bathroom.

There was no ignoring it now. Everything became painfully clear.

And written in red.

Literally.

The bathroom looked like someone had went knife happy on the place—or rather, over the sink. The shirt dangled from Luca's clenched fist as he dared to step closer to the mess, reading the words that had been hastily scrawled on the mirror that faced him while he took in the bloody mess in the sink.

A knife sat on the rim. Half on, blade hanging over the edge. Balancing dangerously … like the woman who put it there, he knew. Holding on, but barely. Blood still red on the blade.

In the mirror, he read Penny's bloody words: *Sorry, this is on my terms now.* He had the distinct feeling the message wasn't directed at him, and yet, it still stung just the same.

Luca started moving a little faster, then. While he raced to put everything together—to figure out how he went to bed with Penny only to wake up alone with a bloody bathroom next door—he managed to shove his shirt down over his head.

Maybe he could catch up with Penny ... wherever in the hell she went. And deal with whatever reason for her disappearance, too. Punching his arms through the sleeves, he went in search of his hoodie and jacket but—

Bang. Bang. Bang.

"Penny, open up! *Penny!*"

Luca's stride came to a stop just beyond the bathroom threshold as the noise became louder.

"Penny, open this goddamn door right now!"

Not that Luca needed more confirmation that Penny had disappeared the night before after she let him fuck her and slept tucked into his side, but the noise outside the hotel room did exactly that for him. He didn't even have time to figure out how that made him feel or what it meant that she left.

Again.

It wasn't the same as the last time.

He knew that.

It still ... hurt.

The banging came again—*louder* and harder. The hint of desperation in the familiar voice calling through the thick hotel door made Luca think the man didn't want to believe what was happening, either.

He recognized the man's voice even though he had only heard it once before. Cree. Given their first meeting, he couldn't exactly forget the man.

"Penny, come on—open the fuck up!"

Luca almost missed it. To his right, the flicker of the laptop screen, he almost fucking missed it because he was distracted by the bloody mess behind him, and the unwelcomed visitors barking at one another between hitting their fists against the door. He could have blamed the fact he just woke up, too, but now he was wide awake so that didn't work.

Nonetheless, Luca saw it.

He watched as the screen of Penny's laptop flickered—the cursor jumped from one side of the page to the other, tabs closing and opening, pages scrolling downward fast before flipping to another one. He didn't even have the chance to blink. He was watching, in real-time, as someone hacked Penny's laptop.

The only good thing about it?

He could see what they saw.

Probably the same thing Penny had been looking at before she set the laptop down and walked away from it the night before. The last thing he saw before the laptop's screen went entirely black was an image and a headline.

He was only able to read the name in the headline: *Allegra Hatheway*. Except he knew that woman—the one in the image at the top of the article before the screen blanked out—as Allegra *Dunsworth*, Penny's mother. Once, he sat at the same table as the woman while lawyers worked out the final details of an estate that was split between two beneficiaries.

Penny and her mother.

But he knew a lot more about Allegra through his years of tracking down every scrap of Penny's history and proof of existence that he could find. It wasn't a lot. It was just enough to tell him that there had never been anything good between the two.

That was all he knew.

So *why* was she looking up her mother?

And why did she leave when she found her?

Those were answers Luca didn't have and wouldn't have the time to figure out. At least, not at the moment. The yelling from outside the hotel room brought him back to reality and out of his self-pity in a flash.

"Open the door or I am breaking it down," he heard called.

Well...

Time for him to go.

It took all of two seconds for Luca to realize what Penny had done and why there was blood in the bathroom. She told him once that The League could find her no matter where she was. He bet the blood wasn't the only thing she left behind for them to find. Might they find a tracking chip at the bottom of the sink drain?

He didn't plan to find out.

How would this situation end for him if Cree—and whoever was with him—broke down the hotel door just to find Luca in there alone? Fuck, they already threatened to kill him. He wasn't about to give them another reason to see it through.

He did like being alive.

Even if he didn't know why.

Luca was just beginning to scale the ledge of the hotel room's small veranda when he heard wood crack as the door was kicked in. Lucky for him, it wasn't the first time he had to make a quick exit ... or take an unconventional route of escape.

Unluckily for the people in the hotel room below Penny's, too. Because the naked couple—the redheaded female riding her partner on the bed facing the veranda down below where Luca landed—certainly hadn't expected him to dart through their hotel room with a quick, "My bad!"

The woman shrieked, scrambling off her partner and grasping for the sheets that really did nothing to hide her body. The man only swore.

"Nice tits, though," he called over his shoulder.

4

They didn't even have time to react. He was already exiting their smaller hotel room before the two even fully understood what had happened. The hallway was empty. He had no idea what was happening above his head a floor higher or if this plan of his would even work.

If he could call it a plan.

Could he if he didn't know what he was doing?

Likely not.

What did it matter?

Luca doubted running would work for him—Nevada wasn't his territory, after all. He didn't have connections, didn't know the streets, and on top of that, still needed to get *out*.

Would it work?

Probably not.

Fuck him if he wouldn't try, though.

Where are you, Penny?

That was the real question.

The entire fucking problem, honestly.

• • •

Luca already had a familiar number dialed, and the cell pressed to his ear with the call ringing through when the remaining man in the airport bathroom finally left. *Without* washing his hands—disgusting prick.

Not that Luca had time to focus on that. Naz picked up his best friend's call in less than two rings, but that wasn't surprising. How many weeks had he gone now without even a text to Naz to explain what was going on?

Too many.

Even he knew it.

No doubt, the conversation wasn't going to end particularly well but if Luca needed help, then he only had one person to go to for it, really. Naz. That was it.

"*Where the fuck are you?*"

The first words out of Naz's mouth the second he picked up Luca's call. Scrubbing a hand down his face, irritated by the thick patch of facial hair that had started to grow out since he'd been without a razor for too damn long, Luca tried not to sigh.

Tried being the keyword.

He failed.

"I'm … in Nevada," he muttered.

"What—"

"With Penny—or I was."

Silence answered him back.

He waited Naz out.

"*What?*" his friend snarled.

Like a record on repeat.

"I don't have long," Luca said, not realizing how true that statement would actually be in just a few short minutes. "But I found her, man. I don't have time to explain everything right now. We went from New York to Nevada—now she's gone again."

"But you were *with* her," Naz replied.

It wasn't even a question.

Luca swallowed hard. "Yeah—"

"And you didn't tell me."

Anger clung to his friend's words. Luca understood that all too well even if he didn't have the time to indulge whatever Naz felt about the news he had just dropped on him without warning. Welcome to Luca's life—that shit was a regular thing now.

"*Point is,*" Luca said, trying to get the conversation back around to what was important, "she got me here, but then she left. And now I think she's got people after her, Naz. Except they're probably after me, too. I've got thirty minutes before I'm jumping on a flight. Better to be back in New York than here, no doubt."

"You were with her and didn't tell me."

"*Naz.*"

He knew good and damn well why that was the thing Naz wanted to focus on. The entire reason why Luca stood where he did boiled down to the fact his friend *asked* him to find Penny in the first place. He'd done that. And didn't tell Naz.

"What does that mean—she *left?*" Naz asked. "How can she leave, Luca? The girl is already *gone.*"

"Woman," he corrected just because that was the only thing his stupid brain decided was most important to say. "She's not—"

"Luca, what is going on?"

God.

He wished he had an answer. An excuse. *Anything.*

Instead, he was left saying, "A lot has happened, man."

"I fucking guess!"

"And—"

"Where is she?" Naz demanded.

Luca blew out a breath, refusing to even turn toward the mirrors where he could see his reflection staring back. Like he needed the visual reminder of the mess this had become and his failures. He felt it more than enough.

"I don't know," Luca admitted. "I basically forced my way to Nevada with her when the people she works for here called her back, but she seemed all right about it. Except I woke up and she's gone, people are banging down the door, and this is all bad. Every bit of it."

"None of that makes any sense."

"It does. I just haven't explained the rest."

Any of it, really. And he wouldn't have the chance to.

Three figures slipped into the airport bathroom, making Luca quiet as he recognized one of the men. The one in the middle with his neat braid flipped over his shoulder and dark eyes nailing into him as if he'd just caught his prey.

"Cree," Luca greeted.

Were they on a first-name basis now? He figured … why not? It wasn't like this situation could end well for Luca, so he might as well do what he wanted while it happened.

"Luca, what's happening?" Naz asked, a worried tinge coloring his tone.

"Nothing—"

"Hang up the phone," the man to Cree's right said.

The one on the left was now pointing a gun at Luca.

All good things.

Not.

"In a sec," Luca replied. And then to Naz, he said, "It's *really* bad now, man."

"Who?"

That was all Naz asked.

Luca simply said, "The League."

"*Hang up the phone.*"

He did.

Not that he wanted to.

Up until that moment, Cree had said nothing. Only the men that accompanied him—men Luca didn't know—spoke. Since he didn't care about the other two, he looked to the man in the middle for what would happen next.

"She's not with you," Cree said, the statement sure and certain.

Nothing else was.

"No," Luca returned, gaze darting back and forth between the two men who stepped closer to him with every second. "Did I give her a head start?"

He didn't need an answer.

Cree's expression was enough.

Yes. They wasted their time chasing him when they should have been looking for Penny. Good. At least, he did something right this time around.

He didn't know why Penny ran.

Or why she left him behind.

He could have been pissed off about that fact—maybe he would be given enough time to think about it—but all he knew was that she *did it.* And she must have had a reason. He bet part of it was The League and why they forced her back to Nevada.

7

"You're coming with us," the taller of the two, on the left, said.

He was already reaching for Luca.

"Don't think so," Luca replied, swinging out of the man's reach.

He just forgot about the other guy. He wouldn't, however, forget how hard the man's punch landed against the right side of Luca's jaw. The hit sent him sprawling to the floor. It was the kick to his head that had stars bursting behind his clenched eyelids, though.

Bastards.

But what did he expect?

2.

RAIN clung to the streets of Brooklyn. Penny avoided the rivulets of water dripping from the eaves of buildings when she dared to stop underneath one as best she could.

The black windbreaker she wore did nothing to keep the wetness from seeping through to her clothes and skin underneath. Despite the chill in the air and the raindrops plastering what white-blonde strands of her hair managed to escape from beneath the jacket's hood, she didn't shiver.

Really, she barely felt it at all.

The discomfort was a comfort. Something else she was used to now. A constant sense of unrest—that nothing was *right* or *good* in a real way. A little bit of water wasn't going to make it any better or worse.

Right?

Penny's gaze swept the quiet Brooklyn street, thankful that the rain had decided to fall despite the weather forecast giving only a fifty-fifty chance of showers. It cleared the streets of almost everyone who didn't need to be on them for one reason or another. With the sun starting to fall beyond the view of the high buildings, darkness had finally begun to creep through the streets.

She felt safe.

Or *safer*.

At least, to be out and about like she was. With barely twelve hours on the ground in New York, Penny had to start moving fast. Part of her plan had been put into motion the second she opened up the safe in her hotel room. It was where she kept several sets of fake identification, a burner phone—one The League didn't know about—and cash she stacked up. She was running on a limited timeline to get certain things done before someone came looking for her.

Someone like The League.

Or The Elite.

If they hadn't already.

Penny was a lot of things, but stupid wasn't one of them. She was neither ignorant, nor arrogant. Certainly not enough of one or the other to think that her decision to go AWOL from her handlers would be met with sighs of resignation and little else.

And *shit*.

The Elite was already hunting her. Might as well make it worth it.

Stepping out from under the entrance of an apartment building, rain splattered against Penny's face as she started her walk again. Cabs were an option if she cared to hail or call one. There was something to be said for walking, though.

Like the fact it let her *think*. She hadn't been doing that enough lately. Well, not for herself, anyway.

Time to do that.

It wasn't as though Penny was just walking to walk—she did have a purpose for being on the streets of Brooklyn in the middle of a cold rain while the sun crept lower and lower with every passing minute. That purpose became clear when she slipped into an alley two blocks away from the last place she stopped.

A car waited there.

The two-door Lexus coup flicked on its lights—once, and then twice, as was agreed upon—illuminating her wet figure in the mouth of the alley. Penny wasted no time slipping further down the alley to the passenger side of the car. Had it been less wet outside, she wouldn't even have bothered with getting inside the vehicle.

Instead, she slipped into the passenger seat and shoved her hood back to expose the fishtail braid flipped over her shoulder that kept *most* of her hair out of her face. The guy sitting in the driver's seat didn't even turn to give her a hello, let alone a look.

"It's in the back," Carson told her.

"Everything?"

"Anything you asked for. I made a list."

Penny rolled her eyes, but smiled, too. "You made a list?"

"You made it clear when you called that this was important. I didn't want to miss anything. Not really good for business, you know?"

She did.

All too well.

Penny found the black duffle bag in the backseat like Carson promised. The independent contractor didn't really have a specific job—he was known to do many things as long as the pay was good and came through. He'd do it without much talk, and he didn't sell information when the chance was on the market, so to speak. She only knew of the guy through other assassins at The League who used him on occasion when in the New York area.

Or Jersey.

Vermont, too.

Carson was flexible.

He also wasn't *owned*. By anyone. Penny liked that a lot more.

Dropping the duffle bag on her lap, Penny yanked open the zipper and spread the top apart to see what was inside. Carson hadn't lied. A pile of burner phones, a small laptop, phone cards and more stared back at her. Sticking her hand into the bag, she moved things aside to find the wigs she asked for. There was also a case of FX makeup, a forty-five millimeter and nine with ammo and a silencer … and finally, antibiotics, a few knives, and a particular obsidian blade with a soft touch handle setting on top of new cargo pants and other black clothing.

Penny closed the bag. "It's all there, thanks."

Carson shot her a look, his tattooed hands never leaving the steering wheel when he asked, "Did you expect anything different?"

"Some of it was unusual."

Like the makeup. And the specific knife she had wanted.

The man only chuckled, asking, "Yeah, I thought so, too. What, are you going to war or on a stage?"

"Maybe both."

Anything was possible now.

In the inner pocket of her windbreaker, Penny pulled out an envelope that was only a little damp from the rain. She passed it over to the man in the driver's seat. His payment that he took without as much as a thank you, not that she expected acknowledgment for their business together.

This was how it worked. They saw nothing. Knew nothing. Said *nothing*.

But just in case …

"If anyone asks," Penny said when she reached for the door handle to exit the vehicle, "you didn't see the white ghost in New York. It won't end well for you if you bring up my name to anyone. Understood?"

Carson lifted one shoulder, unbothered but still recognizing that she warned him. "You know, I don't usually work with people who make it a habit to threaten me, Penny."

So be it.

Except …

Penny laughed as she stepped out of the vehicle, calling back into the man, "I'm not the one you'll have to worry about seeing the threat through, though. Keep it in mind."

There were always worst monsters waiting in the wings. Penny was only one of them.

She closed the door. The last thing she saw from the man was red taillights as he pulled out of the alleyway. That was fine with her.

One thing done.

She was one second closer to ending it all …

• • •

The motel room Penny rented in the Bronx wasn't much to look at. Peeling wallpaper with a faded flower design gave the single room—and attached bathroom—some color, at least. The brown, shag carpet had been laid at least three decades before she even existed. God only knew the things these walls had heard and seen.

That was about all she could say for the motel.

Then again, the place was booked by the hour. She was probably one of the only patrons in the place who paid for several days upfront which should have said enough. Nonetheless, she avoided focusing on the stains on the carpet never mind pulling the sheets off the bed. The old furniture had seen better days but the single table, chair, twin bed, and three-drawer dresser all served their purpose.

She'd stayed in worse.

Hell, she'd been raped in worse.

At least, she was out of the rain, had a place to sleep, and there was a decent diner down the street when her hunger became enough of an annoyance that she had no choice but to deal with it. The motel hadn't required identification to book the room when she slapped down an extra thousand dollars to cover any damages.

Shit.

They could keep the money.

Maybe spruce up the room.

Penny wouldn't come looking for it, anyway. And if she could help it, then she wouldn't bring any problems to the motel, either. After all, the entire point of her getting a room was to use it to stay out of sight. No paper trail. She left nothing behind for someone to use to find her.

Since she didn't have anything else to do, Penny had at least taken the time to open the duffle bag from Carson to look through the items inside properly. Her wigs were now hanging from wire hangers on the shower's metal bar to keep them in decent shape should she need to use one. All the makeup that she might need to change her appearance had been set out on the table alongside three pairs of folded black jeans and matching tank tops. Not that the weapons needed to be cleaned, but she took her time with the gun, silencer, and even the knife just because she could.

What was time?

She had too much of it.

For now.

Keeping busy, even if it was only arranging her things and attempting to settle into the motel room for however long her stay would be, was something she could do. Actions she could control. A way to keep her mind from traveling elsewhere.

To keep her heart from hurting.

It always hurt, though.

Always.

Was it all a bit much? Not really. It was, however, exactly what Penny needed. The League had done more than teach Penny how to kill while giving her the chance to change history ... even if it had taken her entirely too long to figure out the past never went away. They had also given her the ability to take care of herself.

In every way.

Mentally.

Physically.

In *business*.

Having already discarded the burner phone she used to contact Carson, she went ahead and picked a new phone from the pile on the dresser along with one of the cards to activate it. If the man followed her directions—and she knew he did—then each card *and* phone had been purchased from different locations. Despite burners being incredibly hard to track, it wasn't actually impossible given enough time and the right hacker to do it.

Penny didn't want to take chances.

Every single time she used one of the phones, it would be destroyed after. Including this time.

From the pocket of her black jeans, she produced a folded piece of paper that had barely made it through the day's rain. The edges tore at her rough handling, but she didn't care because she didn't plan to use the number written inside again after today.

The thing about politicians?

Anything could be found with little effort. Including their addresses, home phone numbers, and even the names of the schools where their children attended.

Penny only cared about one of those—the phone number to the home where her mother had apparently moved in with her soon-to-be husband, the New Jersey senator, Gilles Tracey. Though they apparently lived in Jersey with the senator's two daughters, they also kept a home in New York and frequently traveled between the two states.

Or, so Penny learned through her searches of the internet. *Anything* could be found ... if someone looked hard enough.

Activating the phone and minutes on the card took little time, and before long, Penny had punched in the number. She put the phone on speaker and held it in front of her as she paced the short length of the motel room while the call rang through.

Once.

Then twice.

A third time.

She honestly didn't know what she expected—getting the number had been a last-minute decision, and not one she really thought out entirely. So much about her mother and the last several years of her life hunting the woman and anyone connected to her had been carefully planned events. Nothing was left to chance.

The thing was …

Penny wanted Allegra to see her coming, now. Nothing else would do.

"Tracey residence—Joesph speaking," came a male voice through the speaker.

Penny almost hung up.

Almost.

She didn't think her mother would actually pick up the phone. She bet the senator had a whole house full of employees to handle every aspect of his daily business. That was before Penny factored in the people her mother probably had on hand.

Nothing about this would be easy.

She already knew it.

"Is Allegra home?" Penny asked opting to just … *see.*

"Ms. Hatheway is upstairs in her sitting room. Give me a moment—I'll put you through. Who am I speaking to?"

"An old friend."

The man didn't even question it.

A click sounded on the phone before a ringing started again. This time, it only rang twice before the call was picked up.

The feminine voice that answered the call was unconcerned and blasé in tone, but the sound of her mother saying hello still felt like a knife raking down Penny's spine.

"Hello," Allegra greeted.

Penny dragged in a slow breath.

Allegra waited one second, and then another before saying again, "Is anyone there?"

"Do you think about me?"

Silence answered back.

It actually made Penny smile.

Then, her mother sucked in a hiss before saying, "Penny—"

She didn't get more out.

Penny wouldn't let her.

Nothing was on Allegra's time anymore. She controlled nothing about Penny. It took years to figure that out, but here she was.

"Did you see me coming?" she asked.

A squeak echoed on the other end of the call, as if Allegra had jumped out of her chair. The woman's next words came out sharp and stinging when she said, "You little bitch—do you know the mess you've caused us? You are *dead*. How long do you think you can last before we find you?"

Yes, she knew.

Too well.

She regretted nothing.

It had to happen.

"I only need to stay ahead of you, actually," Penny returned. "What's left of your organization now, Mother? Every move I've made has taken something else from you, hasn't it? There isn't very much left. Is The Elite even capable of going up against me now—or someone else, for that matter, if you step on the wrong toes trying to get to me?"

The League, she meant. Not that she would say it. That would simply give her mother information she might not otherwise have. Penny wouldn't play *that* game. Just this phone call was dangerous enough.

And she only had one thing left to tell Allegra. Little else really mattered, and she refused to give the woman any more of her life or time than she needed to. Even in her death, Allegra Dunsworth would only get what she deserved and nothing more.

It was all Penny could promise.

The only thing she guaranteed.

"The white ghost is coming for you," Penny told her mother. "Watch for me, Allegra. I'll be seeing you."

Penny ended the call as her gaze found the clock on the motel room's wall. Directly over the bed, it was the only thing on the walls. The second hand kept ticking. A lot like the beats of her broken heart that smashed against her ribcage because just talking to her mother was enough to damn near unravel everything that kept Penny sane.

Tick, tick, tick.

The sound of the clock echoed in the back of her mind. It continued counting down the seconds until she could finally finish this. One after another. She watched the time go.

What choice did she have?

3.

Luca

OVER the years, Luca occasionally found himself in … precarious situations. For a lack of a better word. Situations where he didn't think there was any way out. Yet, he always managed to do exactly that in the end.

He wasn't sure this was the same. Never mind if it would end the same way.

At least, Cree and his men hadn't bothered to do more than tie Luca up while they delivered him to the compound in the middle of the Nevada desert. He didn't have to wonder where he was when he had already been there once—The League's home base. But that was where the good side of things ended.

Luca's prison stared back at him from where he sat in the corner of a room with cement walls and floors. Dampness coated his lungs with every breath, and the shivers crawled over his body the more he tried to get comfortable.

Or warm.

He was going to be lucky to escape this without catching a fucking cold, let alone with his *life*.

It didn't help that his arms had been tied at his back with zip ties connected to a metal bitch link protruding from the cracked cement. He couldn't even use his hands to warm his own body, and the hard floor wasn't doing anything for his aching muscles.

Every part of him hurt. The rusty metallic tang of old blood lingered on the back of his tongue every time he dared to lick his chapped lips.

The worst part?

Luca couldn't tell time—he had no idea how long he'd been there stuck in the cement room with no windows to see the rising sun to say another day had come and passed. Only a bare bulb with a long, thin chain hung from the ceiling to provide light.

It had yet to be shut off.

Even when he did fall asleep—though he seriously doubted it was for more than a few minutes at a time with the way his mind felt slow and *tired*—he could see that goddamn light in his dreams. It was just there … shining bright in the background like it was fucking taunting him or something.

What was happening?

That's all he wanted to know.

Anything.

He'd take anything now.

Luca was close to drifting back to a hellish dreamland—if one could even call it that—when an echoing beep had his eyes jerking open. Metal clinked, then, and in the next second, the double doors at the far end of the room with the squeaky hinges opened without the prompting of the man who waited on the other side of them.

Over the doors sat a camera. Pointed and trained on him, the red blinking light over the lens was yet another thing that continued to haunt his waking dreams.

"You're looking … well," Cree murmured when he stepped inside the room.

Luca had every urge to tell the man to go fuck himself, but he held back. *Barely*. Cree could have been less kind given Luca's current circumstance, but he wasn't. Not intentionally, anyway.

He didn't bother replying to Cree's first comment, instead asking, "Have you found her?"

Penny, he meant.

He didn't need to say her name. He bet every single person in this building—however many there were—knew exactly why he was there.

Cree came to a stop in the middle of the room still ten feet away from a bound Luca. At least, they let him keep his boots even if they did rip the laces out of them. His ankles weren't tied, so that was something to be thankful for, too. If only he could get his wrists undone and out of the strange room, then he might be able to—

"No, we haven't," Cree finally replied, interrupting Luca's thoughts. "Do you feel betrayed because of what she did?"

Luca's brow dipped. "What did she do?"

Cree raised a single, thick brow high. His dark eyes nailed into Luca like he was trying to decide whether the man had lost his mind or was just stupid.

Frankly, even Luca didn't know the answer to that one. Not now.

"She brought you here," Cree clarified, "and decided you could be used as a good distraction for the rest of us while she headed off to do her own thing. As for you, well, you followed right along."

Huh.

"That's what she did?"

That's why Penny let him follow her to Nevada?

He didn't think so.

Not entirely.

"That's what she did," Cree echoed.

Luca shrugged—as much as he could in his constraints. "No, I don't feel betrayed. I don't feel anything at all."

17

Well, partly.

He felt too many things, really. Betrayal simply wasn't one of them.

"I can't say the same," Cree admitted quietly.

Luca didn't acknowledge the man's words. He figured it was probably better if he didn't. It wasn't like he could pretend to know the bonds Penny shared with these people—if she had any at all to speak of, that was. Nonetheless, there had to be something. She spent over five years with these people. Someone felt *something*.

That was only human.

The longer Cree stood there watching Luca where he sat in the corner on the floor, the more he fidgeted. While he'd only been vaguely aware of the restraints on his wrists before, as he'd become used to them to an extent, now the plastic was biting into his skin in the worst way.

He talked just to distract himself from thinking about it, asking, "What is she doing, anyway?"

Cree sighed. "Going after her mother."

That had Luca interested.

"What?"

The man passed him a look; the neat plait of his long braid belied the dirty scuff marks on his black cargo pants. "The Elite—her mother."

Luca still didn't understand. Or maybe his tired brain just wasn't letting him put it all together. Either way, he opted to say nothing at all. Better to keep one's mouth closed and let someone think he was a fool than open it and prove it.

Right?

"You don't know, do you?" Cree asked.

Luca swallowed hard. "I know *some*."

"But you haven't put it all together."

"In a bit of a situation at the moment. I like to prioritize things I have to worry about if you know what I mean. Forgive me."

That almost had the man smiling. Or smirking, maybe.

"Don't feel bad," Cree told him, "no one can understand Penny or what she went through. Not really because no one should have to know the horrors she faced. And not once, but again and again. To get the full picture, you would have to go back in time … and that's just not possible, Luca Puzza."

He had the distinct feeling that Cree was trying to tell Luca something without actually *telling* him, so to speak. But with little sleep, hunger aching deep in his belly, and an unknown future waiting beyond the doors of the room he currently called home … well, he just couldn't pinpoint *what* Cree wanted him to know.

"You were her last hope," Luca said. "This was it—wasn't it? For what she was trying to do, whatever she ran from years ago, this was the end of the road. The last place to go."

Cree's throat flexed, and his jaw tensed like he wanted to say something, but he was forcing the words back. Eventually, the man replied, "Apparently not ... look at her now."

What did that mean?

Cree turned to leave, but Luca was quick to speak up and stop the man, asking, "What are you going to do with me now?"

A sharp gaze looked back.

Luca was still unafraid.

"At least let me know—so I'm ready for whatever it is," he told the man.

Cree's broad shoulders lifted almost carelessly. "We haven't decided yet."

He didn't ask why.

He already knew.

The League still thought he might be able to help them. *Somehow.* Maybe with Penny, or perhaps with something else. Who knew? Either way, they weren't about to throw him away like trash when he could still be useful.

It was smart business.

Bad for him, though.

But didn't they know?

"All I ever tried to do was help Penny," Luca said at Cree's retreating back as the man left the room, the beep resounded again over top the door, and they started to close him back in. "It never worked."

That didn't mean he would stop trying. It wasn't his style.

• • •

"Where are you taking me?" Luca demanded.

His captor—face hidden by a black mask—said nothing as he continued shoving the barrel end of his rifle into Luca's back. The action forced him to keep walking through the many corridors of the compound. All in silence, too, because other than the man's gun driving into his spine every time the guy wanted him to speed up, shut up, or otherwise, he wasn't getting anything from the man.

Fucking hell.

The long, empty hallways of The League's complex still felt cold and impersonal. Like the walls and every closed door had secrets to tell—ones he wasn't privy to. The entire place seemed full of ghosts that he couldn't see, and there wasn't a single part of him that liked it, either.

Luca didn't recognize the path he was made to take with the armed guard still at his back. They didn't pass a soul on the way as they climbed two stairwells to an upper level of the building where *finally*, he started to hear something. Low, murmured voices that he couldn't discern well enough to distinguish between the number of speakers let alone the conversation as a whole.

He didn't know what it was until he was walked right into the middle of it, though. One last jab of the rifle to his back, right between his shoulder blades, and Luca stumbled—still tied at his wrists—into a large room.

Walls of screens stared back at him. The handful of men inside the space stopped talking just long enough to turn his way. They—including Cree, and four other men Luca didn't recognize—turned their attention back on the man standing behind the massive metal and glass desk that dominated the space.

They were still talking.

Luca just wasn't interested.

The screens had his attention now. And the shit plastered on them. Images of faces—people—made up a pyramid. Some faces had been crossed out with large Xs while others were left untouched. It was the two faces at the very top that had Luca starting to see the bigger picture.

The Elite, he knew.

Who else would it be?

Some of the images with Xs were recognizable faces. Murders that Luca could easily connect back to what he knew about Penny's business over the last few years. But only because *he* had been looking for her. Someone else might not see it, but he sure as fuck did. She had been taking them out one by one.

Then, he happened.

Or rather, he caught up to Penny.

What changed?

Allegra and the woman's father sat at the very top of the pyramid.

That was the thing he missed ...

Allegra Dunsworth stared back from the screen. Her image held so much similarity to Penny that at first, it was shocking. It wasn't the first time he saw the woman, but it was the moment that he realized what Penny must see every time she stood in front of a mirror.

Her mother.

A monster.

Staring back at her.

Finally, the conversation between the men in the room caught Luca's attention enough to drag him away from the images on the screen.

"Another pet project for Cree to get under control," the man behind the desk said. "At this point, I'm starting to think taking these on aren't worth the trouble they cause us."

"Dare—"

The man behind the desk held up a single hand, his steely gaze looking over every man in the room except Luca where he still stood just a couple of feet inside the doorway. "She was given directions, Cree. An *order*. One she didn't follow. We only have one option, and I can't help that you don't like it. She's put The League in danger of The Elite being able to trace and track us like we've been doing to them for years. Every single member of this organization is an *asset*. Ones we cannot afford to lose given the nature of this work, and you know it."

"That doesn't change that she's only doing what we told her she would—"

"She was given orders!"

The shout silenced the room.

The man they called Dare regained his composure quickly, and finally glanced Luca's way when he said, "Circumstances and loyalties change all the time. A by-product of the business. You don't need me to tell you. She's gone AWOL. We react accordingly and protect what we've built. This is your mess to clean, Cree."

Were they talking about *sacrificing* Penny?

Dare pointed at Luca, saying, "Including that mess there."

But what did that mean?

Luca wasn't given the chance to ask, let alone speak before the man behind the desk nodded at him, drawing every gaze in the room to him when he said, "And *you*."

"What about me?" Luca asked.

At this point, what did he have to lose? He only needed to get *out*. He just didn't know what *out* meant or looked like.

"A request to make an offer for you has come through from New York," Dare said, folding his arms across his silk-covered chest, making the fabric of his button-down strain from the action. Then, he added, "We're at least willing to *hear* the offer from the Donati family."

"An offer—"

"For your life."

Well, then.

4.

"HE blames me for this."

Luca looked away from the glowing lights of his favorite city down below only to find the man who had spoken wasn't even looking at him. Directly in front of his seat was another where Cree had taken a spot when they boarded the private jet hours ago. The flight attendant on board opted to stay with the pilot after the assassins on the jet made it clear they weren't interested in being attended to for the flight's duration.

He might have liked something.

Nobody cared to ask.

"Who?" Luca asked.

Cree's dark gaze shifted subtly from the window to Luca, then to the man a couple of seats back with—Dare—and then back to the window again. It was so fast it was almost like it hadn't happened in the first place. "My ... partner."

That had Luca's brow furrowing while he put together what the other man was trying to tell him. It seemed like Cree did that a lot—talked just enough to be interesting while letting those around him figure out the rest for themselves.

Luca couldn't say he liked it.

This was, however, the most conversation he had been able to gain from anyone since leaving The League's grounds. He wasn't about to waste it. Despite their flight starting to come to an end with New York below them, he figured Cree wasn't the type to talk just because he could. It always seemed to serve a purpose.

So, what was it this time?

"And he blames you." Luca's statement didn't gain him anything from Cree. The man acted like he hadn't even talked, let alone repeated what he had already said. He tried something else. "For what, exactly?"

Cree arched a brow, never looking away from the porthole window. *Well ...*

"For Penny, you mean," Luca said when the man wouldn't. "That she went AWOL from her handler—*you*. So all of this comes back to you. Everything she does from here on out is basically on you, right?"

Cree smoothed a palm down his long braid as he leaned back in his seat and stared straight ahead at Luca. This time, he didn't look further down the jet at the man behind them in another seat when he said, "He blames me for doing this. Or what she's done, I suppose. He wants robots.

Unfeeling *machines*. But broken people only end up breaking other things more often than not. What purpose does that serve? He says they're my pet projects. I get attached, call them *mine*, make them different and better."

"And that means you—"

"Try to fix them."

"Even Penny?"

Cree swallowed hard, the suit he'd thrown on for the trip making the man look all the more uncomfortable in his seat when he replied coldly, "Especially her. It worked. Look at her now."

Right.

Except no one could *look* at her. She was gone.

All the while, Luca was still wondering if tonight would be his last night alive. Fun times.

The plane's descent finally hit the point where the pressure in the cabin changed enough that it wasn't quite comfortable. Luca thought his conversation with Cree was mostly over when the man didn't offer anything else. He went back to staring out the jet's window at the lights below because even planning something like an escape at this point felt useless.

"He blames me," Cree murmured, although this time to himself more than to Luca, and neither man acknowledged the repeated words. "And he's not wrong."

• • •

Luca wasn't sure what he expected when the jet touched down at the New York airport, but seeing his father standing next to Cross when he exited the plane certainly wasn't it. Apparently, whatever offer the Donati crime family had to make for his safe return by The League wouldn't be waiting one second longer than it had to.

Was he grateful?

Of course.

He just hadn't expected them to be waiting ... *right there*. The very moment he stepped off the plane.

Luca kept his composure while the team of men dressed in black—from their cargo and tight, long sleeve shirts to even the gear strapped to their bodies—surrounded him when his feet hit the tarmac. Dare and Cree, the only two men in the bunch that hadn't dressed like they were ready to go to war, headed the group and came to a stop in front of the private hangar where Luca's father and godfather waited.

There was something to be said for being treated like you were ... a ticking time bomb. Each of the five men appointed to him watched his every move. Like the next one would be his last, but as if they still expected him to *try*.

23

Luca was way out of his league here. Even he fucking knew it. That was why he had no intention of stepping out of line in any way that might jeopardize whatever chance he had to make it out of the situation alive. If living the life he did had taught him anything over the years, it was that self-preservation was something a person needed to survive their world.

Or maybe that was just him.

"Step forward," came the muffled order at his back from one of the men in black with his face partially covered by a black skull bandana. The butt of his rifle came forward like he was going to jab Luca in the back but fuck that noise. He'd had enough of that in Nevada, and he wasn't doing it again.

Luca moved ahead, through the two men at his front that parted to let him pass, so that he was able to stand slightly behind, but off to the side of Cree and Dare. Zeke and Cross waited with the men of The League, and only turned back to continue their conversation once Luca was in their sights.

He knew what he looked like.

All too well.

The assholes might have cut the ties on his wrists and gave him back his jacket before they left Nevada, but he was still in a goddamn state. He needed several hours of sleep, clean clothes, *and* a shower. His haggard appearance was probably only aided by the fact he hadn't shaved in far too long, he was due for a haircut to manage the high fade cut that had grown out. The beating he'd taken—more than once during his time with The League—left with him a couple of bruises that hurt more than he cared to show.

No doubt, those brief few seconds his father and Cross had to see him told the men more than Luca would when this was over.

But he could handle it.

All of this.

It was all secondary to the fact Penny was still *gone*, and he was sure an entire team of assassins would soon be hunting her down on top of the people that were already looking for her from an entirely different organization. At least, for Luca everything else was secondary to that. He couldn't say the same for everyone else on that tarmac.

"Is even the suggestion of talking about what to do with the other situation on the—"

"It's nowhere near the fucking table," Dare interjected, stopping Cross from saying anything more. Luca had finally stepped out of his thoughts just long enough to realize he could hear some of the men's conversation above the wind in front of the hangar. "The contract is clear, Mr. Donati. *If* your property remains under the supervision of The League while maintaining business for you, it is at our discretion to make final calls regarding disobedience. Especially at this level."

"I just think there are other ways to deal with Penny than—"

"There isn't," Cree said, his words loud and clear but still somber. Like he'd accepted the decision that had been reached—one Luca wasn't entirely clear on—but he didn't like it all the same. "The last two years we have seen her reach higher and higher levels with each kill she made inside The Elite—she was nearly at the end. To have the chance to end it taken away when and like it was ... she won't return to business with us. Or even you, for that matter. She's fulfilling her own purpose. It's beyond us, and it always will be. There is no going back."

Cree stiffened at the sound of Dare's sigh, but other than that, silence and stillness passed between the four men.

Luca was finally catching up.

Again.

Dare and Cree spoke to Cross about Penny and her business with The League like *he* was also a part of it. As if he had a right to know because the details were ones that should have already been understood.

He felt stupid.

So fucking angry.

All the time he spent trying to find why Penny left or even, who helped her ... adding it on top of the dozens of questions that piled up when he found her entangled with The League, and it was all for nothing. The man who made all of that happen had been in front of him—or pretty damn close—from the start.

Cross.

His godfather.

Naz's dad.

He thought, *of course.*

But also, *why.*

"We're here for one reason," Dare said, the first to break the silence and restart the conversation. "I was gracious enough to at least allow you to make an offer ..." The man's gaze slid Luca's way before he added, "And I understand why, so do so before I change my mind."

Cross dragged in a hard breath. "You won't even entertain Penny?"

"No."

"Cross," Zeke said.

Now, his father was looking at him. The worry in Zeke's eyes was clear—bright like the sun on a summer's day when the sky was wide, and *blue.* If he regretted anything, it was that. Sure, they had their issues, but Zeke was still his father at the end of the day. He tried to keep that in mind now.

"I know," Cross told his best friend, before turning back to Dare. "Fine. Luca is returned—he is off the market and not to be touched otherwise. In return, I don't interfere with your business in New York or make any calls to make it harder for you to do said business."

Wait—

"They're going to go after Penny," Luca said, the words bursting from his mouth before he could stop them. They had to understand what it meant to do what they were doing here. "You're going to let them—"

"Exactly that, yes," Cross told him, nodding once. Then, to Dare, he asked, "Does that work for you?"

"It does," Dare replied.

That was that.

The men in black backed off. Dare and Cree had already turned to head for the private hangar while the team of men who had been watching Luca followed behind. The three men—including him—that were left outside said nothing as the wind picked up again.

It sounded like a whine. Or maybe a howl. It reminded him of the sound an animal made when it was in pain. He hated to think that was God's way of warning him of just how much this would soon hurt.

• • •

Luca didn't complain when he was dropped off at the front entrance of his apartment building the night before, but only because he was two seconds away from falling over his own two feet. Exhaustion was a real thing. He wasn't, however, impressed at the fact someone decided to knock on his door before the sun had even risen in the sky.

He was still trying to rub the sleep out of his eyes, and drop the bad attitude, when he ripped the door of his apartment open to see who was waiting on the other side.

Cross.

In nothing but boxer-briefs, Luca was in no way ready to wake up, let alone invite someone into his place, but his godfather stood on the other side of the threshold like that was exactly what he expected to happen. He couldn't say that was going to work out for the man. Even if Cross did look like he was ready to start his day in a three-piece suit with his hair slicked back and shoes shined.

Luca held tight to the door, not opening it further or moving an inch when he said, "You need something?"

Because after the night before and the things he learned, Luca couldn't say he was willing to provide anything Cross might need. The only good thing about not being made—at the moment—was the fact he didn't actually have to answer to this man, anyway.

Cross gave him a look, and then the door Luca was keeping mostly closed against his side. "Are you going to keep me out here in the hallway?"

"Considering it."

"Luca—"

"I'm busy. Places to be, Naz to see," Luca said, shrugging.

Cross cleared his throat, sucking hair between his teeth after before he muttered, "Naz is busy, Luca."

"Too busy to see me?"

His best friend?

Right now?

Luca didn't think so.

"Actually," Cross said, folding his arms over his chest and looking at Luca in the way he would when he was a kid. But that shit didn't work on him anymore—not when this man did it, or when his own father tried it. Three decades of life under his belt made him immune to most of that nonsense, and he couldn't say he was sorry about it, either. "Naz doesn't even know you're back in the city yet. It all happened fast ... I used that to my advantage."

Yeah.

Luca bet.

"Something else you're hiding, then," Luca noted.

Cross didn't like that.

He didn't even try to hide it.

"Hey, watch your fucking tone with—"

Nah.

"I'm good," Luca said, stepped back from the doorway and closing the door on his godfather, telling him at the same time, "Keep in mind, I'm not *your* man. Not made, remember? If I don't want to do this, or anything else, with you, then I don't have to."

The door was about to click shut, but Cross's next words stopped Luca from letting it close entirely.

"But if you want to help Penny, you're going to have to do everything you don't want to do and more," he said.

Luca hesitated.

He didn't open the door back up right away. In fact, his hand tightened around the handle so much that his knuckles turned white as he considered those words and what they might mean. The lump growing in his throat certainly didn't help matters, either.

"And I know," his godfather added, "about you and her."

That took Luca an extra minute.

Maybe two.

Cross didn't mind the silence because he used that time to his advantage to keep talking. "Thank The League for keeping me informed—part of their obligation to the old contract. See, I put a lot of money on the table for Penny to be able to do what she's done in these past five years, and that gave me ... certain rights to information about her business."

"Did she know that you knew—"

"Yes on some things. Maybe not on others. I wasn't given the information to use it against her, if that's what you're asking. Sometimes, it was just good to be informed."

"Naz doesn't know that me and her—he doesn't know shit about it yet."

"I figured," Cross murmured. "But the better question is what do you know?"

Luca swallowed hard as he swung the door open further. Leaning against the doorjamb, he crossed his arms and muttered, "A lot of it. Where she's been, what she's been doing ... everything happening now."

"And her mother?"

He nodded once.

That was enough for Cross.

"Then you should also know what it means for her mother to do what she's done in recent weeks," Cross said.

Luca couldn't help the harsh sigh that passed his lips as he scrubbed a hand over his freshly shaven face. At least, he managed that and a shower the night before. "I'm starting to figure it out, yeah."

"She's put herself back in the public sphere in a way that she hopes will protect her—or at least give her a wider space for safety—from Penny while she attempts to rebuild what remains of the organization she controls with her own father. Allegra Dunsworth is *not* an easy target, Luca. Penny knew it when she first went into it and—"

"Penny is in a bad position."

"Especially because she decided to go AWOL now. Anyone," Cross said, giving Luca a look, "*anyone at all* close to her or even attached to her name is at risk of being put on The Elite's radar. A way they can get to her, if needed. The Elite is bigger than just North America—there was a reason she was overseas for as long as she was."

"Except she needs to finish what she started," Luca replied.

Because that much was clear.

Why else would Penny do this?

"I did what I could," Cross said, flipping over one hand when he added, "and the rest is on her. The better question, is what does that mean for *you*. What are you going to do?"

Was that why his godfather showed up—just to ask that question?

Luca did think so.

"I'm going to help her. The same thing I've always done," Luca said.

It was the only thing he knew how to do. It was the *how* he planned to do anything at all that he hadn't quite figured out yet. Unfortunately, he was running on limited time to get that shit worked out, and he couldn't do that standing at the front door of his apartment.

If there was anything he learned about Penny in all the years he spent chasing her, it was that she knew how to disappear.

"But I can't help her standing here with you," Luca said, turning back to his apartment and ready to close the door again. "You already know that, *zio*."

It'd been years since he called Cross that.

He heard the man's sigh before Cross said, "You can't tell him, Luca. Naz, I mean. You can't say a word about my involvement with Penny or The League. He'll learn in his own time, but not because you told him."

Well …

"I can't promise that," Luca replied.

He didn't promise anything.

Not anymore.

5.

BY the time Luca did make it to Naz's house just outside of the city it was well past dinner time, and the sun had already started to set. He didn't exactly plan to be that late but shit happened. Like a phone call from his mother which ended up morphing into a chat with his father as well despite the man being on the tarmac the night before when Luca arrived back in New York.

After that, he needed an entire drink—and then a second—to compose himself before he was even ready to consider leaving his apartment. But then the landlord showed up with a fucking attitude because Luca hadn't been around to drop off his rent for the month. As if he didn't typically pay several months ahead, and this was the first time he was late.

If it wasn't one thing, it was another. The saying rang true—when it rained, it poured. Maybe he was just getting used to the world dumping trash on him because Luca took it all in stride. Or, he tried.

He was still late to show up at Naz's—too late, really. Even he knew it. He certainly didn't expect to walk through the front door and find the house lit up in all corners with life bustling all around, but he didn't expect to find the quiet, somber mood he did, either.

Nor did he think his sister would be sitting on the entry stairs with a mug of hot coffee between her palms, staring at him like he owed her something. Maybe he did, even if he didn't want to admit it. It wasn't just Naz that he had been keeping secrets from lately. Although, the choice not to tell Roz the truth about his business looking for Penny hadn't been one he personally made. That was something Naz made the final call on—Luca hadn't argued the pros or cons.

Not his wife, not his life.

Right?

"Naz told you, then?" he asked Roz.

It took his sister a moment to respond. Her fingers flexed around the ceramic mug while her throat bobbed with an audible swallow. A good sign that she was angry and trying *not* to show it. Family was important—it was a rule that had been drilled into the two of them for longer than Luca cared to remember. A good rule, though. At least, it allowed them to consider their words before they spoke them aloud to one another.

"I'm mad at him, too," Roz whispered.

Holding back tears, he knew. He could hear it in her voice, but that was also why she wouldn't look up at him. She didn't want him to see the water in her eyes.

"I'm mad at Naz, too," she said, louder the second time but still sure and clear. "Because he told me years ago that you had stopped looking—there was no hope. He didn't have answers, and I should *move on*, Luca. And then what, I turn around and find out that's all you've ever done—but *oh*, you found her, too. You found Penny, but she's—"

"I'm sorry," Luca murmured.

Roz shook her head, a sad laugh leaving her frowning lips as she gathered her thoughts. He let her. What else could he do?

"Naz says it's bad," Roz eventually said, the first between them to break the silence.

"He's not lying."

"Well, forgive me if it's hard to trust—"

"Roz," Luca said, stepping closer so that he could kneel down in front of his sister. She still didn't want to look at him where she sat in her shorts and tank top pajama set on her stairs, but she eventually did. "You've known Naz for as long as you've been alive—don't ever say you can't trust him. You know that's not true."

She sniffled but nodded once. "Still mad."

"Be mad if you need."

"Yeah, okay." Roz lifted one shoulder and looked upward when she said, "He's in his office. We're … or *he*, is doing a thing. Letting me be by myself for a bit."

"How loud did you yell?"

Because Roz *never* yelled. She was a lot like their mother in that way— Katya Puzza didn't raise her voice unless it was the last option. And when she did yell, everybody knew shit was about to go down and to get out of the way.

"Pretty loud," she said softly, ashamed.

Luca gave her a small smile. "Sometimes, we need that. Guys, I mean. Draw the lines, Roz, and fucking hold them."

His sister didn't respond, but Luca figured she didn't need to. On his way past Roz to climb the stairs and find Naz, he dropped a kiss to the top of her head. She could be mad, like he said, and eventually … she wouldn't be. Perhaps then, they could really talk about *this*. The entire fucking mess. Or maybe they wouldn't say anything at all. Whatever she needed, he was good with it. He owed her that, at the very least.

Luca passed his godson's bedroom on his way to Naz's upstairs office. He was sure he saw little Cross tucked comfortably under his blankets, but he didn't dare linger at the doorway for too long. The boy should sleep, and just because Luca hadn't seen the kid in weeks didn't mean he had any right to wake him up when it wouldn't be him putting Cross back to bed.

Naz was barking into the phone when Luca did walk into his office. He barely even passed his best friend a look as he told whoever was on the phone to, "You better get that fucking shit done—if I have to come down there and make sure you do it, I *will*, but I promise you won't like what comes after, Lou. Don't test my kindness. It's quickly running out."

He slammed the phone down to the receiver with enough force that a frame fell over on the desk. Naz didn't even bother to correct it before his angry, sharp gaze turned on Luca.

"Dad handled it, then?" Naz asked.

Luca raised a brow. "Handled what?"

"*You.* I figured you were in some kind of shit when you called, so I got him on the phone. I didn't have much to go on but here you are. Things worked out I see."

Luca swallowed hard. "Yeah, you could say that."

Or he could say how Naz's father was one of the reasons why they were in this entire situation in the first goddamn place, but—

"I'm sitting boss," Naz told him.

Luca stiffened. "What?"

"There wasn't any warning. Dad stepped back at tribute a couple of weeks ago, and put me on the spot. It wasn't like I didn't see it coming—he already had me doing more shit than I should have been. So yeah, you're looking at the boss of the Donati family. This life doesn't stop for anything, Luca."

Right.

Not even when the world did.

Luca knew it better than anyone—he'd grown up watching his father sacrifice his personal life and time to the mafia time and time again. Even when his wife would beg him to make time for her and the kids when shit was really bad, Zeke ended up saying the same thing.

Famiglia first.

Family business always came first.

Luca just couldn't help but wonder if Cross putting his son in his place to handle the business side of things was circumstance—because it was time for it to happen—or something else ... like maybe another way to keep Naz busy and out of his father's private affairs. Say, what was currently happening with The League and Penny.

Naz didn't give him a chance to voice what Luca knew or even his thoughts before he asked, "What do you know—what *happened?*"

"You want it all, or cliff notes?"

Naz arched a brow. "Probably both."

Well, then ...

"That's fair," Luca murmured.

"How long were you with her before … what, she went missing again, right?"

"I think they didn't give her a choice."

"They?"

"The League."

Naz nodded, and scrubbed a hand down his jaw. "And you—but you were *with* her."

"For a little while. By chance, really. I didn't find her because I did anything different. It just happened. I was fucking *lucky*, but it was also fast … it wasn't a good situation. She already had people hunting her down before I even came on the damn scene, you know?"

"No."

Luca blinked, surprised at how sharply Naz said the word. "I—"

"No, I *don't* fucking know! And you know why—because you didn't tell me! Beyond the fact that you were doing this for me, that you were looking for her *because* of me, you didn't even have the decency to let me know—"

"It's not that simple, man. None of this was simple."

"Fuck you."

"Naz—"

"*Fuck you.*"

The unspoken *I said what I said* lingered between the two men, hanging heavily in the air like a poison that would easily kill them both. It was the Donati way, Luca knew. Donati men were all the same when it came right down to it, and Naz was no different than his father at the end of the day. Their stubborn streaks were legendary.

He knew when to push.

Or not.

Naz waved a hand, saying, "Start over—from the beginning. I want to know how this happened. I want to know why you're standing here right now and she's not. Tell me everything."

Well …

Luca would try.

He didn't skimp on details—mostly. He started from the beginning like Naz wanted him to, from that night at the hotel, until the point the familiar man showed up to demand Penny return to Nevada. He kept out the personal shit, and he respected Cross wishes about keeping his involvement on the down-low but that was only because Luca didn't know how to approach it yet.

Or if he even should.

Nonetheless, he gave Naz the bones and most of the meat of the story. From The League, to even The Elite. He didn't stop there, even going as far as explaining how Allegra Dunsworth fit into it, her upcoming marriage to a respected senator, and what Luca had learned over the past couple of days. The longer he spoke, the more irritated his friend became.

With him, certainly.

But also with everything else.

It was expected.

Naz raged for a bit. Luca let him.

At the end of the day, only one thing really mattered to him now.

"I need to find her," Luca said when Naz finished his rant about people keeping shit from him just because they could. His friend wasn't *wrong*, he just didn't have the time or concern to handle that when other things needed his attention. Things like *Penny*. "She's already got whatever remains of The Elite—or whoever is working for them—looking for her. Now, she's going to have an entire team of assassins from another organization hunting her down, too."

Naz fell into the chair behind his oak desk. "It all comes back to her mother, doesn't it?"

"Like one messy, vicious circle."

"And The League—"

"I got the impression that because they don't think they'll be able to get the situation under control with Penny being AWOL that they're going to handle it in a more … permanent way."

"Kill her, you mean. Just say it."

Luca dragged in a shaky breath. "Yeah. It's just her … whatever she's trying to do right now, she's out there doing it alone."

He didn't like that.

He couldn't have that.

"They can't risk it otherwise," Luca added.

"Risk *what*?"

"Her boss. The League, Naz. What they *are*—what they do, you know?"

"Not really."

"Yeah, me either."

But here he was.

Trying.

No one could ever say Luca didn't try.

"Her boss," Naz said, circling a finger in the air when he added, "go back to that. Who is her boss if not the organization she's—"

The lie slipped from his mouth before he could stop it. Another to add to the growing pile that he would eventually have to deal with. Luca would, just not now.

"They didn't say," Luca said.

He swallowed that proverbial pill. It wasn't easy.

"This is bad." Naz leaned back in the chair, staring at the ceiling overhead like he was waiting for the heavens to open up above him. "Worse than I thought—she's a dead woman walking. Think about it."

"It's not going to happen, though," Luca said, wanting his friend to know that at the very least. "This isn't over, Naz. She's not *dead*. Not yet. And she won't be if I have anything to say about it."

That had his friend sitting straighter in the chair, and eyeing him.

He avoided Naz's gaze when he said, "I know the Donatis can't go up against an organization like The League and come out of it relatively unharmed, but she might not need that, either. And I've got a leg up—I know she's going after her mother. I only need to be where that bitch is and work from there."

"You've gone from tracking her to protecting her, then?"

Luca's jaw clicked when he clenched it. "Who else is doing it?"

Naz kept watching him.

Considering.

"Anything else you wanna tell me about Penny—and you, maybe?" Naz asked.

He should.

He *wanted* to.

Luca had no reason not to tell Naz what had transpired between him and Penny since he found her again. And *shit*, he wanted to tell someone. Anyone, because then it might make that real. The new loneliness in his heart was a real fucking thing he couldn't escape. The constant worry and emptiness that wouldn't leave him alone were driving him insane. It wasn't fair that he'd dedicated practically so many years to something—or someone, rather—that he wasn't sure would ever be his.

It only recently dawned on him that Penny *did* feel like his, in a way. As if that shit wasn't terrifying enough. He'd always felt something for Penny, but it wasn't the same now.

Obsessive.

Clawing.

Constant.

"Not yet," Luca settled on telling Naz, "but I will. Soon."

"But there is something to tell?"

"There's something."

One less lie between them.

Didn't that count for anything?

"I just need a place to start, and I can find her again—go from there," Luca muttered more to himself than to Naz.

"You don't know, do you?"

"Know what?"

Naz pushed his chair back just far enough that he could open a drawer in his desk. Yanking out a newspaper, he slapped it to the top of the desk and nodded at Luca to take a look. "That right there—published today in the *Times.*"

Luca's confusion only lasted as long as it took him to get the newspaper in his hands. Naz already had the paper open and folded to the story on the third page—an entire article dedicated to exposing Allegra Hatheway as Allegra Dunsworth. Maybe *exposing* wasn't the right word as the journalist simply connected the dots of the woman's history, her former husband's arrest for child pornography, and his subsequent death. *There was a suggestion that the charges facing Preston Dunsworth had only scratched the surface*, the journalist had written in black and white. Holding back only a bit.

But it was enough, he knew.

Enough to do damage. To ruin a reputation. To fuck shit up for certain people—like Allegra. Or even her current fiancé who certainly couldn't afford a scandal of this kind with his high profile nature and politics in the way.

"What are the chances," Naz asked, "that story dropped now just because?"

Luca glanced up from the page, meeting his friend's stare. "I don't believe in coincidences like that."

"Me, either. And if this is coming out, chances are, it's not going to be the last thing we see on the topic."

Right.

"Penny is feeding information to the papers."

Or to someone.

It would have to be her.

Who else would—

"Maybe she's giving people a place to start looking because then she controls where everyone else is while she's somewhere else," Luca murmured.

Naz shrugged. "It's smart."

But messy.

And now Luca needed to figure out how to look through any distractions Penny put out to find what she didn't want him to.

Luca could tell Naz was still pissed at him. Since they were kids, nothing had been off-limits between the two. He didn't wonder *why* his friend felt the way he did. "I know you've still got shit to say to me about all of this," he told Naz, "but we can get back to that at another time. Because right now, I'm running out of time to find Penny. If someone else finds her before I do … listen, nothing good is going to come from that, man."

Naz sighed harshly. "She's not the same, is she?"

"It's been five years, Naz."

"I know, but … she's not the same, is she?"

Luca thought about that.

And what he could say.

Penny was …

Better.

Amazing.

Dangerous.

To him, she was enthralling.

He settled on telling his friend, "No, she's different than she used to be, but it's not a bad thing."

6.

Penny

THERE was something to be said for returning to a place where it all began … at least, in Penny's world. One might think the start of her life—good or bad—had been at the New Jersey home tucked deep within a gated community where her parents kept a permanent residence until her father found himself locked behind bars for his misdeeds.

All the horrors of the three-level Victorian home were hidden by tall, green edges and a manicured lawn. The luxury vehicles that used to sit in the driveway, and the picture-perfect image her parents presented to the world kept suspicion at bay from anyone who dared to look beyond the pretty surface to find the cracked layers underneath.

And even so, that had been where her life began.

Right?

Wrong.

Penny's life started somewhere else. Or what she considered to be the start of it, anyway. Was life really a life worth living if someone didn't know what love was, or how to love? Was life at all important when one wasn't really *living* it, only existing?

That came later for her.

Learning how to live, that was.

It was also every reason why instead of returning to New Jersey … she found herself back in New York. Or specifically, walking the bumpy, dirt path—one of many—that connected the forested area behind Rozalynn and Nazio Donati's home and their rear property.

Was it too close for comfort?

Yes.

Was she being foolish?

Absolutely.

It was … more days than she cared to count since she went AWOL from The League. She didn't doubt for a second that her former handlers already had a small army looking for her. She was a situation they needed to get under control, and they would certainly try to do just that by whatever means necessary.

It also changed nothing.

Penny was done following orders that would not serve her best interests or the interests of the people who she had done this for in the first place. She wasn't going to make it easy on The League—or anyone else that dared to get in her way—while she finished her business with Allegra Dunsworth.

She shouldn't have come back to Naz and Roz when they would undoubtedly be the first place The League came to look for Penny. Very few others knew her past like her handlers did, though, so she was willing to take the risk. It wasn't like she planned to stay for long.

And yet, despite it all, Penny couldn't help but come back one more time before everything changed again. Before *she* changed everything.

She didn't plan to show herself or even walk up and knock on the backdoor. Her adoptive family would never even know she had been there after she left. They deserved better than a random appearance and another disappearance. She threw their world into upheaval once just by being there and then again when she left without an explanation. There was no good reason to do it to them again. Even she knew that.

No, she just wanted to … see them.

Or their home, rather.

Remind herself why she was here in the first place and what brought her to the point that she was willing to … give it all up.

Her protection from being who she was. The family she desperately missed. A career that had allowed her both healing and retribution for the wrongs done to her. The chance to start over, or to *be* someone else, even.

To learn what came *after* …

All of it and more.

Penny was giving it up—or any chance of it by doing what she had done, really.

Still, as she lingered at the edge of the forest, ten feet beyond where the treeline ended on Naz and Roz's property, she couldn't help but think it was still worth it. For them, and their life, even if it was one without her.

And for her, too.

For her peace of mind. Something she never had—not while her mother still walked and breathed.

Soon, Allegra wouldn't.

Penny needed to start over first. Go back to the beginning and *remember*. To know that for a time, before all of this happened, she was happy. Or … she was starting to learn how to be happy in her own way. Until her mother ruined that, too.

Some things never changed …

Lost in her thoughts and still staring at the only home she had ever known, Penny was too distracted to hear the crack of twigs from her left. That was, until a little voice said, "Hey, Penny."

Whether it was the shock of someone saying her name, or just the fact that they had managed to sneak up on her in the forest behind Naz and Roz's property, it still earned a reaction from Penny. She hadn't heard the approach from her left until the new voice joined a silent conversation she'd been having inside her head while the memories raced for attention in her mind.

Despite her years of training to stand calm and steady no matter the situation, she let out a yelp and fell backward when she stumbled over an exposed root of a tree. The white strands of her hair made a curtain over her eyes as her palms hit the ground to catch her fall from turning into something much worse.

A quiet, child-like laugh rang out in the forest. The sound was almost musical and a total contrast to the way her heart thumped loudly in her chest.

"Sorry," her new companion said, "I didn't mean to scare you."

Penny didn't bother to get up, or even fix her hair. Instead, she pushed sideways and came to sit right on her ass, so she could stare directly at the guest who had joined her in the forest. He was maybe three and half feet tall, not quite four, *if that*. Dark hair. *Soul-deep eyes*. She found familiarity in the softness of his boyish features. Even the way his grin tilted a little more on the right side in a smirk she had seen time and time again.

She didn't need to ask his name.

She already knew.

"Cross," she said.

The boy shrugged. "Well, everybody calls me *little* Cross when they think I can't hear. I don't like that very much. But since Grandpapa doesn't like being called Senior, I have to deal with it. Or that's what he said."

His words were clear. His sentences, smart. For his age, anyway.

"And you are, right—*Penny*, I mean?"

She stared at the boy, blinking as if he might disappear in the next minute. She was still trying to figure out why in the hell he was even in the woods. Where were his parents? Was this something he did on the regular? *Hell* ...

Penny hadn't seen his face since he was six months old. Not once in all the years since she left had she even been graced with a picture of the boy as he grew. She always wondered, of course ... did he keep his father's features, or change to look more like his mom?

She missed a lot.

About him.

His first steps.

Those first words.

Even his first day at school.

"You don't talk?" Cross asked. "Ma says you were always quiet."

She swallowed hard, knowing what she *needed* to tell the boy because she wasn't even supposed to be here in the first place. "I don't know who you think I am, but I'm not—"

"Yeah, you're Penny. I have pictures."

So sure.

And *true.*

God.

Penny dragged in a quick breath. "You didn't scare m—"

"Yeah, I did," he interjected again, seemingly unbothered that he kept interrupting her. "Sorry. It *was* kind of funny, though."

She couldn't help the smile fighting to get out. He was quite the kid. It only killed her more.

"You know they're looking for you, right?" Cross asked.

Penny wet her lips. "How do *you* know that?"

"Uncle Luca came back. I heard Papa say he was lying. There was *a lot* of yelling."

"You call him your uncle?"

Cross lifted one shoulder covered by a leather jacket that looked *strikingly* like one his father would have worn years ago. The children's Doc Martens on his feet matched the whole vibe. The one thing he didn't have was the slicked-back hair, but the wild strands of his black hair looked better all crazy anyway.

"He's my godfather, too," Luca added. "So …"

Penny knew.

"And you're supposed to be my godmother."

"Yeah, I am," she admitted quietly.

"*Supposed to be,*" the boy said again, "because you're not here. You never were. And even though everybody else knows you, I don't."

"You knew me. Just for a short time."

That didn't satisfy the boy at all.

"Yeah, well. Not the same." He sighed hard, glancing through the trees at his house when he said, "I like it out here. I'm not supposed to go past the trees, but … well, I do what I want."

Penny laughed under her breath. "We all do."

"Not like me."

What did that mean?

"You're smart, aren't you?" she asked.

Cross pressed his lips together as he considered that before saying, "Yeah, but not like my papa. Different."

"How?"

"He's … smart-*smart*, you know? Numbers, and books, and *things*. All the things. Universe stuff. I see people and just *know*."

Penny's brow dipped. "Know what?"

Cross looked back her way, those soul-deep brown eyes of his piercing and *apprehensive* and knowing when he replied, "Well, everything, Penny."

She thought … *no way*.

"Really?"

The boy smiled half-heartedly, saying, "It's a lot sometimes. People lie, I know. When people hurt, I see it. Ma says it makes me special. Papa says … it is what it is."

"And what do you think?"

"I think you ask about me because you don't want me to ask about *you*."

And just like that, Penny knew he was telling her the truth.

"I should go," Penny said, pushing up from the ground and brushing the dirt from her backside at the same time.

Cross glanced her way, frowning openly. "Remember when I said I didn't know you?"

"Yeah."

"I did know enough *about* you. I know you must have loved me before you left and made my ma and papa sad, right? Because you made me something to keep—something I would always have." Cross shuffled his feet against the dry ground, kicking up some dirt and dead leaves in the process when he muttered, "I mean, nobody makes a song for someone else just *because*."

Some did.

Not Penny.

"Of course, I loved you."

Dark eyes of a five-and-a-half-year-old lifted to meet hers when he asked, "Then why did you leave?" Cross tipped his chin higher, that sharp gaze of his looking Penny up and down without pause. *Considering*, she knew. Considering her. Waiting to find her lie. Like maybe he could sense it before it even passed her lips. *Could he?* "I'm little, even though I don't like it, but they know I'm not little, too, in some ways. So they're careful when they talk. But they still do or I still hear it. You were with my parents for more than a year. You said you loved me—they loved *you*, I know. And then you left. *Why?*"

If only Penny dared to close her eyes, she imagined that she could pretend this was a conversation between two adults. Certainly not one between a grown woman and a five-year-old boy. It was a strange thing to hear wisdom in the voice of a child. She had to wonder if that was how people felt talking to her as a child that had seen and knew things that were far beyond her comprehension.

"That's not an easy answer," Penny replied in a whisper.

"The truth is always easy," Cross replied, folding his leather-clad arms over his small chest. There was something to be said about being stared down by a child. Especially when it felt like that child was also judging you. "Because people lie—*all the time*. Everyone does it. But they always have to think about it, make sure it *sounds* right … it's a choice to lie. Like Uncle Luca says, shit's a process."

Penny coughed out a laugh alongside muttering, "He says *what?*"

Cross rolled his eyes. "He says a lot of stuff. That one is right, though. The truth just *is*. Telling it sometimes hurts, or changes things, but it is still the truth. Right?"

"You see things in a very black and white way, don't you?"

"Kind of."

"Is it easier that way?" she asked. "Easier to understand why you get to be this way … and everyone else is the way they are, too?"

Honestly curious, she waited for his reply.

The little boy blinked, surprise darting over his young face for a split second. "No one's ever asked me that before."

"No?"

"No."

Penny shoved her hands into the pockets of her black windbreaker, telling him, "Maybe because they don't know how—they can't understand anyway."

"Maybe. And it's not easy. It just is."

Penny didn't point out how he said the same thing about the truth. Whether he knew it or not, yes, he did deal with his strange uniqueness in a yes or no, black or white manner because it was easier for him than delving deeper.

It showed his youth. Possibly one of the few things that did. What he lacked in actual age and experience, he simplified things down to just *being*.

Cross lifted his brow and smiled, a flash of arrogance showing in the action that almost had her laughing when he added, "But you still didn't tell me why, and I didn't forget."

Smart kid.

In a lot of damn ways.

"Because I had to," she said, knowing all too well it wouldn't satisfy him, but it also wasn't a lie. "I left because I had to."

"That's …" Cross's brow furrowed. "Well, *why?*"

"Because it was the right thing to do. The only thing I could do."

"Do *what*, though?"

"Leave," she replied.

Cross let out a huff, gaze narrowing in on her again with a new gleam. "I know what you're doing."

Penny grinned. "Yeah?"

"Saying the truth."

"But?"

"Without details," he said, defeated.

She only shrugged.

Fair was fair.

Her godson might have card tricks of his own—although being able to read people at his age was way more amazing than just a *card trick*—but she had a few, too.

Cross shook his head. "Uncle Luca told them you were different."

That made her pause.

All over.

Penny turned to stone at just the mere mention of Luca. She had been content to come back to this place, say goodbye and *hope*, and then leave it all behind if that's what came of her choices. She'd forced herself to stop thinking about the people she kept leaving behind, too. Sacrifices had to be made, after all.

That didn't stop it from hurting.

Cross observed her in silent stillness, waiting for a reply from her that wouldn't come. It couldn't. "He likes you a lot, too."

Penny's throat flexed when she managed to ask, "What?"

"Uncle Luca. When people miss things—things that mean *something*—their eyes change. More distant. Like they're looking at something far away. Something I can't see. You did what he did when he told them he found you. But you did it now because I talked about him. See, same thing."

This kid was … something else.

She also couldn't afford to stand there and keep talking to him even though every single molecule in her being wanted to do exactly that. He was amazing. It took a single conversation with the kid to realize just how much she had missed out on where he was concerned.

"I really should go," Penny said, moving a step deeper into the forest. The same way she had come.

The shout from behind her made her next step hesitate.

"*Cross!* Get back to the house, son! Time to eat!"

Penny's head snapped to the side, gaze darting over her shoulder through the trees to find the form of a man coming to stand on the rear porch of the three-level home. Like his son, she hadn't laid eyes on Nazio in as many years.

Not much had changed.

He was older, yes, but his playful grin as he called for his child still felt like a welcomed sight to her.

"Cross!" he called again.

The little boy just a few feet away looked her way with a shrug. "You're gonna leave now, huh?"

"I have to."

He nodded once. "Yeah, you keep doing that to people, I guess. *Leaving*."

Penny blinked away the veil of tears that shrouded her vision. "I don't want to, though."

"*Cross Nazio Donati*—time to eat, kiddo!"

As if on cue, Cross's stomach growled. He didn't even look sheepish about it.

"The interlude—the part of the song that repeats, right?" he asked her.

She smiled. "Yeah, what about it?"

"Mine feels like a hug."

Penny stilled.

He couldn't know that …

It wasn't possible.

"It does," he said again. "It feels like a hug when I hear it. I feel the same. Light at first. But then it tightens, *muffles*. Like arms wrapping around me, bringing me closer, getting warmer and tighter."

"I composed a lullaby for you. That's all."

Cross kicked at the dirt when his father called his name again. "Yeah, but with a hug. Right?"

"The way I thought a hug should feel. If someone made one with music. If I could hug you through mine."

Not that she ever told anyone that fact.

"Okay." Cross turned back toward the house. "That's what I thought."

"Cross, are you in those damn woods again?"

Penny sucked in a sharp breath at the sight of Nazio strolling down the steps of the porch and heading their way. Toward the woods.

"I have to—"

Penny didn't even get to finish her sentence before the boy had turned back around. He darted for her, his small arms wrapping around her middle. The hug was light at first, and then it tightened with warmth.

"Please don't tell them you saw me," she whispered, hugging the boy back. "I only want to help them, okay?"

If she could have stayed right there in that moment with a piece of her past cementing her between *then* and *now*, she would have. Forever.

"I won't tell." Cross peered up at her when he took a step back and let her go, asking, "You'll come back, won't you?"

She chose not to lie.

"I'm sure gonna try."

7.

Penny

ALLEGRA was being smart.

Too smart, really.

Penny didn't think for a minute that anything the woman did was just because. Every decision Allegra made had a purpose. From staying out of the spotlight for many years to announcing a marriage to a man who was a public figure. All of it did something for Allegra at the end of the day. It served her needs.

Hunting her when she was underground had been difficult—and the focus for Penny had always been taking out other Elite members until it was time to go after the ones sitting at the very top. However, it hadn't been entirely impossible.

Allegra's newest hat trick, the marriage to the New Jersey senator, made everything harder. Or at the very least, it made Penny's job difficult. That job being to *kill her*. Well, it wasn't hard to do that, per se. The difficulty came from the fact there was no clean way out. The woman was surrounded at all angles by people protecting her.

But Allegra wanted attention, right? Why else would she decide to marry a man that she knew would cause her face to be splashed across the papers and evening news reports?

Oh, *yes*.

Because she stupidly thought that would also protect her. That there was no way anyone would come after her because it wouldn't be a clean hit with all the cameras watching. How would someone get away without scrutiny after it was all said and done?

Allegra made shit hard.

Penny decided to … *help*.

"Jocelyn," Penny greeted, taking a seat at the two-chair table in a quiet cafe in downtown Manhattan. She wouldn't usually travel so deep into the city—but especially not where there were so many suits around. Something about it made her uncomfortable in a way she didn't care to explore, but sometimes, it couldn't be helped.

The journalist sitting on the other side of the table glanced up with wide eyes at the sight of Penny. Her hair was the color of wind-swept wheat, tied back into a neat ponytail at the nape of her neck. The way she tried to fix the waistband of her pencil skirt and then her black heels, one of which she beat rhythmically against the table leg, spoke to her nervousness at simply having Penny nearby.

She should be nervous. All of this was dangerous.

"What are you doing here?" Jocelyn demanded, her brown eyes darting from Penny to the windows that overlooked the bustling street outside. No one was paying them any mind, but that didn't stop the woman's paranoia from showing itself. Penny expected that. "You told me—"

"Everything is fine. I wasn't followed. No one even knows where I am."

The reassurance didn't stop Jocelyn from swallowing hard enough for Penny to hear it across the table. The woman drummed her manicured nails to the table, the white tips reminding Penny of the first time she approached the journalist at her favorite nail salon with a story for an article—and proof on hand—that she wouldn't be able to refuse.

She hadn't.

Two days ago, the article published on the third page of the *Times* newspaper detailing the crimes Allegra's last husband—and Penny's dead father—had been convicted of and how his wife walked away without a scratch despite the suspicions and proof of her involvement in his acts. Penny dared to use one of her phone cards and a new burner to watch the response unfold in real-time in online forums and other venues.

If Allegra wanted attention from the media, then Penny could give it to her. It might not be the kind of attention her mother liked or wanted, but nobody said this would be fair.

Or easy.

Penny tried to keep it in mind.

"Still," Jocelyn said, the shake in her voice clear to Penny even if the woman didn't acknowledge it, "you can't just *show up* whenever. At least give me a little warning."

"So then I might give someone else a warning, too?"

"What?"

Penny lifted a brow. "Never mind."

Jocelyn's gaze darted back to the windows, and then she scanned the cafe around them, obviously looking to see if someone was watching them. It was then that Penny had a realization about the woman's paranoia.

"You think someone is following you."

It wasn't even a question.

Jocelyn's stare came back to Penny in an instant, and she shook her head. "I don't *see* anyone but sometimes I notice similar cars, and familiar faces I can't place. And—"

She stopped all at once.

Penny couldn't have that. "*And?*"

"My door was unlocked yesterday. When I got home, I mean. I-I never ... *ever* ... leave it unlocked. I have a cat, I don't want her getting out, you know? So, I leave it locked like the windows and—"

"I get it."

"Is someone following me?" Jocelyn asked her.

Penny figured ... honesty was the best policy.

"Probably," she replied. "Which is part of the reason I'm here. Just to tell you that your best bet is to get out of town for a while. Let things calm down—stay far away from any idea that you have a connection to *me*. Keep out of sight."

Jocelyn's dark stare burned bright with new anger. She even dared to lean closer to Penny over top the table when she said, "You didn't tell me this was going to happen."

What did she expect?

Penny handed her the story of a lifetime with the possibility of more should things go a certain way. Beyond that, she'd explained—or tried—the darker truth surrounding the situation and how it could be potentially dangerous to publish it.

"You didn't ask," Penny replied simply. "But yes, I knew it was a possibility that ... *someone* ... might track you after publication just to see if they could connect you to me in some real way. It's nothing personal, just business. They want to find me. You could be a means of doing that which is why I just told you to get out of town. Everyone has sacrifices to make to get a job done, Jocelyn. Even you."

Even if the journalist *was* the sacrifice Penny made.

So be it.

Sometimes, it had to be done.

Penny stood from the table, having said what she needed to, as Jocelyn asked her, "But ... what am I supposed to do now?"

Over her shoulder, as she walked away, she said to the woman, "I told you—*run.*"

• • •

The wind was worse next to the river. Yet, Penny didn't move as she waited for the call to be picked up. With the phone pressed to her ear, she watched the movement on the Hudson from the safety of the shadows she had found.

Thankfully, she didn't have to wait for long.

"Marcel speaking—"

"Do you remember that time I overlooked your side business with that friend from Canada, so it wouldn't get back to Dare when we were doing that job last year?" Penny asked the hacker as soon as he picked up her call. Considering he wasn't supposed to do *any* side business at all outside of The League for reasons related to the entire reason for him becoming a member ... she knew that was the best place to open their conversation.

"*Penny.*"

"One and only."

Marcel paused just long enough to mutter, "I do remember that time, yes. One favor. That's all you get, though."

"Fair enough. It's all I really need."

And if Marcel was willing to do it, then that's all Penny cared about. He would be putting a lot on the line to help her in any way—even if he didn't realize he *would* be helping her against their own people—and The League wouldn't take kindly to that. If they found out, of course.

Computer keys clicked fast in the background. Penny wasn't stupid—she knew what the man was doing. Or, she was pretty sure.

"Are you trying to trace me?" she asked.

"Trying," he admits. "Kind of part of my job right now. No offense."

"Of course, but I'm using a burner, *and* it'll be at the bottom of the Hudson when this conversation is over. Just in case anyone might like to retrieve it, you know."

Marcel cleared his throat, saying, "Thanks for that. Makes one thing easier."

"No problem."

She knew how this game was played. Penny had been on the other side of it for a long time. Now that *she* was the one they were trying to find, she knew all the tricks to stay just beyond reach. As long as she didn't fuck up. Easier said than done, honestly. One wrong step could ruin a lot for her here.

"You know the Hudson really nails you down to—"

"They know where I am. But I am one in millions. Good luck."

"Right," Marcel said in a dark laugh. "The favor? Which I really shouldn't be doing for you, by the way. Every active member in The League is on your file right now, Penny."

"Fascinating. I want a bounty put out with no name attached for who listed it. A million for a successful kill."

"A bounty on who?"

For a moment, Penny hesitated.

Not for long, though.

"On me," she said. "Last known location—the state of New York."

Marcel's clicking on the other end of the call came to an abrupt stop. The silence raged through the telephone, and she understood why. No *sane* assassin put a bounty out on themselves. It was practically suicide. In fact, that was usually the only reason an assassin would do such a thing in the first place. Because there was no other choice.

Well … there was another reason.

Penny found one.

It was still suicide.

"It's going to be a lot harder for the right people to find me when *everyone* is looking for me," she said quietly.

Marcel let out a slow, steady breath before replying, "That's also dangerous."

Yep.

"And a risk I am willing to take."

It was going to make The League and The Elite's job a lot harder to find her when they also had possibly hundreds of rogue assassins flooding New York to deal with at the same time. With everyone and anyone coming out of the woodwork to claim a million-dollar bounty on the white ghost, well … that was an opportunity too good to pass up, she knew. A kill like her on someone's list would make them gold in their world.

No one would say no.

But she had to stay alive, too.

Win some, lose some.

Story of her life.

"I can do that—list the bounty, I mean. And make the payment through your offshore accounts when it's been claimed, too." Marcel's clicking had started up again, adding, "Nothing will be tracked back to you or me as well."

"Expected nothing else. And—"

"One favor, Penny. That's all you get."

She almost smiled.

"Except this is a personal request. Something of mine that I want to be returned. So to speak …"

"I'm not following," he returned.

"I want the files unsealed and dumped."

A pause answered her back. Then, the hacker asked, "What files?"

"You know what files."

Every single image and video of her as a child—each scrap of evidence that proved her sexual abuse and trafficking by her parents. Everything that The League spent years finding and hiding at her behest. It served two purposes—one to help her heal while also erasing her very existence. Or a part of it, anyway.

"I want it to be clear," Penny said, "that girl and the white ghost are one in the same."

"Penny, I can't willingly release child po—"

"They are *my* files. They are my images and videos. Of *me*. Only me."

"Penny—"

"It's my choice, Marcel. Unseal and dump them."

"But … why?" the hacker asked.

Well, that wasn't an easy answer. And not one she planned to give to the man on the other end of the call. It wasn't like she *wanted* people to see those images and videos. She didn't want to give other predators more fodder for their dark and illegal desires. But she also had no other choice.

Penny had to throw as many wrenches into the plans of others as she could—including releasing any and all information about herself that she could afford to without putting her safety at risk. Especially if it hurt her mother and any plans Allegra might have.

Like her marriage. This would certainly make that hard to see through. At least, on Senator Gilles Tracey's side of things. The woman might be able to scare one reporter away, but she seriously doubted Allegra would be able to do the same when Penny's files were dumped and available for public consumption. Not to mention, when those files made their way to the offices of reporters and journalists all over the state.

Eat your heart out, Mother.

It's what you deserve.

"Because I said so—one more thing," Penny said to Marcel as she readied to end the call.

"Christ, what now?"

"How are they doing? The League, I mean?"

"Tracking you."

"Obviously. I meant—"

"You're ahead of them," Marcel murmured. "But only barely. You're both in New York now. Or at least, a team is there. It's only a matter of time, Penny."

Right.

But she just afforded herself some more.

And that's what counted.

One second after another.

It all added up.

8.

"WHAT are you doing right now?"

Luca didn't usually like when conversations opened up that way. It almost always meant someone was going to pile more shit on top of his to-do list, and he *really* couldn't afford more at the moment.

"Depends on what you've got to tell me," Luca said, taking a right turn onto the next block. "And my godson is in the back seat, so keep that shit clean, you know?"

Keys chuckled deeply. "Thanks for the heads-up—Naz Donati's son, right? He's in that fancy fucking private school for gifted youth, huh? Smart kid."

Luca tensed a bit at the hacker's personal knowledge of a side of his life that he had never shared with the man.

Before he could even say anything about it, Keys added, "Sorry, I check out shit about everybody when I'm bored. Bad habit—you start to feel like you can just join in on people's lives when they don't even realize you're a part of it. Know what I mean?"

"Not really."

"It's … a hacker thing. Speaking of which—"

"What?"

"Just listen, things are looking *up* for you," Keys muttered, making Luca remove one hand from the steering wheel to massage at the side of his temple where a headache was starting to form.

The thing about life lately? It was really testing his patience. In every single aspect—including *people*. He took a second to check on little Cross in the backseat, safe in his booster seat while he ate a cup of gelato and watched the city streets pass them by. At least, the kid was happy and unconcerned. But Cross always *seemed* that way. The people around him over the years had learned the boy was always listening.

Always.

And he heard what people thought he didn't. He understood more than people could sometimes be comfortable with—*honestly*. Gifted didn't begin to cover his nephew, but the way the kid's eyes flickered back and forth at passing buildings told Luca he *was* distracted. The conversation happening between the hacker and his uncle didn't interest him at all.

One thing to his favor.

Back to Keys, Luca said, "Things are going to be looking some way for you if you don't stop wasting my time with this conversation, too."

"Hey, be nice."

"*Keys.*"

"All right—I was only trying to make conversation."

"I don't have time for conversation right now, man. I'm running out of time to find her here, remember?"

The hacker on the other end of the line cleared his throat, a more serious note taking a hold of his tone when he replied, "Shit, right, okay. Back to it, then?"

"*Please.*"

"You got it—was going to ease you into this, but that's not going to work. So, I have a ... *friend.*"

Luca's gaze narrowed. "Are you fucking with me *again*—"

"Nah, *listen.* I can count on one hand the number of times Marcel has called me in the last ten years. He's an old friend, shit went bad years ago, and he got out. And I don't know what happened to him, but sometimes I'd get a call. A friend in the business that started where I did—there's a code, Luca."

"Why am I getting an entire backstory here?"

Keys sighed so loudly the speakers crackled in the Bluetooth. "The point *is*—I never asked about what happened because it wasn't on the table. The *code.* If you're safe, that's great. But he called again. I was over here minding my own goddamn business and checking up on that shit about the white ghost you sent me."

"What does this have anything to do with—"

"He wanted to ask a favor—a million-dollar bounty to be listed in New York. He figured since the last known location was here, it'd be better to open the bounty here. Really get the underground moving here while the bounty spreads outside the state. The man isn't wrong, and he wanted to go through my servers to do it because they're the most secure in the state to do it remotely, but that's not the good part."

"What is?"

"Who the bounty is *on.*"

Luca blinked, finally catching up to speed. No, Keys hadn't been wasting his time at all. "The white ghost."

"Yeah, man. So—"

"Did he have her location nailed down *within* New York?"

It was the only thing he cared to ask. The only thing that really *mattered.*

Keys quieted, and Luca had his answer before the man even said it. His heart sunk deep in his gut when the hacker muttered, "Most he could say was she had been in the state for a while and he could pinpoint her at or near the Hudson river in the past two days because *she* confirmed it. And we know that basically tells us nothing."

The urge to punch his steering wheel came on so strongly that it shocked even himself. Luca swallowed back the desire, remembering the little boy still eating his gelato in the backseat. Not that the kid hadn't occasionally seen violent things. It was the nature of their life.

He at least tried to give Cross some semblance of *normal* when he could—a lot like his father had done for him, and Naz still tried to do. Which was every reason why when something came up for business unexpectedly on Naz's side of things, Luca was quick to jump in and take his godson off the man's hands even though he had his own shit going on.

Life didn't relent.

Luca was her bitch lately.

"Wait," Luca said, realizing something else, "*she* confirmed it—he talked to her?"

"Man, I've already said too much. It's ... the *code*, okay?"

"Nothing you know will help me? That's all I wanna know."

"She put it on herself."

"What?"

Keys swore severely under his breath before spitting out, "The bounty. She put it on herself."

Jesus Christ.

The silence stretched on deafeningly as Luca tried to absorb what that meant for Penny. He couldn't even pretend he came from her ... *world.* He only graced the surface with his business through Naz and doing retrieval work over the years. It wasn't the same as the life Penny lived as an assassin for The League. He knew that.

But he wasn't so ignorant that he couldn't comprehend what it meant for her to take a step to put a bounty on herself. A world-class assassin whose moniker had only been whispered about in the tightest of circles for years.

It might take a week for New York to be in a state of chaos as anyone who had the means and motive to see the bounty through mobilized to New York to hunt down the infamous white ghost, but the next few days would be dangerous for Penny to even breathe near an uncovered window where she might be recognized or seen.

"You still there?" the hacker eventually asked.

Luca swallowed hard as his car came to a stop at a red light. "I ... I gotta go."

He had to catch up to Penny.

Somehow.

And his day wasn't over yet.

• • •

Before Naz had even called Luca that day, he'd already been set on a task that needed his attention immediately. Time was running out for him to look into it when he'd gotten word about it that morning through a friend with connections to the journalist that had published the piece in the *Times* about Allegra's history—using both her married name Dunsworth, and connecting it to her maiden name, Hatheway.

He didn't have time to take his godson off Naz's hands—even if it was just for a drive to drop him back off with his mother—but he also couldn't say no. Not when he knew his friend was trying to get as much time with his son as possible while also dealing with the politics of family business as he took his father's vacated seat for the business side of things.

And that was all before Keys called to drop his bomb.

Luca was pulling double-duty and doing so dangerously. He knew it as he leaned in the rear passenger door to hand his cell phone to his godson, telling Cross, "Play one of those games you like—I'll be back in five minutes. *Do not* unlock the car for anybody. Got it, shithead?"

Cross gave him a look from the side. "Got it."

"You better."

"I *do.*"

All that attitude in such a small body. The kid just didn't know what to do with it. A lot like his father, Luca supposed.

"Be good, buddy."

Cross was already flipping through the pages of Luca's phone when he closed the door and pulled out the fob to lock the car. Satisfied somebody wouldn't be punching out the window of his car on a cool day when he was *right across the street*, he darted through slow moving traffic to the line of yellow police tape at the entrance of a large apartment building's parking lot.

Beyond the line of police vehicles that had been parked inside the lot, Luca could see what movement remained at the scene. Which wasn't very much. The lack of a coroner's vehicle or an ambulance told him he had been too fucking late to catch someone—like maybe a reporter—that could confirm what he'd heard happened here in the early morning hours.

"Shitty thing, huh?"

The new voice at his left had Luca turning that way. The approaching security guard with a cigarette tucked between the same two fingers that he used to scratch his bulging midsection nodded toward the cops that were chatting at the rear of one police vehicle.

"They're finally finishing up. It's been a whole day thing. Don't know why when they said it was just a suicide."

Luca stuffed his hands in his pockets, deciding to lie because maybe he *could* get something. "Yeah, a friend of mine lives on the fifth floor. Guess she saw the body this morning. Jumped from the—"

"Twenty-fifth floor, yeah. Some reporter's—or a journalist, maybe?—husband."

"The one that wrote the article in the *Times* that got a lot of attention recently, right? About the senator's fiancée. *Crazy.* Was she there?"

"Nah, they can't find her. The thing about it … people don't usually jump headfirst, but hey, the cops said the place was quiet. Nothing out of the ordinary. And I'm just a fucking security guard, you know what I mean?"

Luca's first thought?

Professionals.

But which ones?

The Elite?

The League?

Someone else?

Anything was possible.

"And sorry," the guard told him, "but I can't let anybody through until they cut the tape. Only residents of the building. Your friend will be here on another day."

Shit, yeah.

Right.

"Thanks, man," Luca said.

For more than he knew …

By the time Luca returned to his car, his mind was already running a million miles a minute. He needed to stop trying to find Penny, and start *thinking* like her at this point. They were beyond the line of just finding her—time had run out for that.

Slipping inside the driver's seat after he'd unlocked the car, Luca wasn't surprised to find Cross had discarded his phone to the backseat. The kid never liked electronics as a distraction. At least he wasn't longer than the five minutes he promised.

"We're gonna go see your mom," he told his godson, getting the car turned on and in gear.

Cross nodded. "Okay. You know she's going to come back, don't you?"

Luca's check of traffic as he maneuvered out of the parking spot came to an abrupt stop as his gaze darted to the rearview mirror. His nephew watched him with the same calm demeanor he always had when he was doing … *that shit.* He didn't even know what to call it. Vibing, maybe. Feeling the aura of the people around him—reading the damn room.

All of it and *more.*

"Who?" Luca dared to ask.

But he thought he might already know.

"Penny," Cross said. "That's what you're doing, right? You're looking for her. I saw her—she promised. She'll come back. But I'm not supposed to tell anyone."

Fucking hell.

Luca swallowed hard, realizing he was right—he needed to think like Penny—as he told little Cross, "Keep that promise—nobody but me, okay?"

"Okay."

9.

Penny

THE rapid flicker of the overhead light setup in the busy, popular Brooklyn club moved to the beat of the same music that vibrated the floor under Penny's combat boots. In black cargo pants and a tight long sleeve in the same color, she certainly didn't *fit in* with the crowd around her, but that wasn't the point. She wasn't trying to blend in with the people when she didn't intend to stay long enough to need to.

Not that it mattered.

She hadn't even come through the front—instead, she used a knife and pick to bust out one of the older locks on a side exit door when the drunks stumbled out of the alleyway long enough for her to get the job done. It wasn't like the security at the front would let her in looking like she did— guns and knives strapped into the holsters at her chest and thighs—and she thought the thirty-dollar entrance fee was a little steep.

But that was none of her business. She wasn't here for any of that.

Penny could, however, see her current target on a platform that rested higher than the rest of the dancefloor. Metal stairs led up to where rope sectioned off the setup filled with red leather booths and black tables. Two men in suits waited at the velvet, braided rope. Their presence and posture was more than enough to tell her there were likely guns under their three-piece suits.

They wouldn't be a problem.

Knowing better than to linger—with a live bounty on her head, even being in a packed club with hundreds of faces all around her was dangerous—Penny headed for the platform VIP section. Unsurprisingly, she caught the eye of the man sitting in the booth alone before she had even managed to reach the stairs.

He didn't stand. His dark gaze didn't show surprise. Almost like ... he expected to see her there.

"Take a break," she heard him tell the two guards who had finally noticed her approach. "It's fine. Go have a smoke, and take him with you."

"But, boss—"

"*Go.*"

They didn't question the order again. Penny wondered, as the two men took the metal stairs down and passed her on the way, how many times they dared to question Cross Donati even *once*. By the look in his eye as he followed their retreating backs, it wasn't very often. So was the life of a mafia boss, or that's what she had come to learn.

The older man—with hair as dark as tar and only a whisper of gray despite the years that had left crow's feet at the corner of his eyes—didn't bother to stand even when Penny stood on the other side of the table from him. He tipped his head to the side, taking in her getup and the long white braid that she had flipped over her shoulder to at least keep it under control for the moment.

"Plans tonight?" he asked.

Penny shook her head. "Being cautious."

"Yes, I suppose you have to do that now, don't you? Comes with the territory of having a million-dollar bounty on your head."

"Semantics."

Cross gave her a look.

Penny only shrugged back.

Where was the lie?

"How did you find me?" he asked. "Tonight, specifically."

"I know the right people. And I'm good at making phone calls."

"And you're here because—"

"Out of respect," Penny told her former boss. "In case you had something to say to me, or you wanted to make a request. I thought it was only fair, considering … well, you know."

"That I paid millions for you to become what you did? That you're offering a single *million* to make it all go away? That every effort we made to make you invisible was completely shot to shit? Or how about even that I've had to lie to my son and—"

"How did you know it was me—the bounty, I mean?"

Cross smirked, reaching forward for the glass of whiskey on the table. He downed half of what remained in the glass in one go and set it back down on the table with a *crack*. "Who else, Penny? Who else would do that the way it was done?"

"I've got a lot of enemies."

"*Now*," he agreed.

"I always did."

The second she made her first kill within the ranks of pedophile rings overseas, she became a target. Each kill she added to the list after the first only added more to her back. It never really bothered her—that was a sacrifice she was willing to make, after all. Better her than … everyone else.

Right?

She wasn't so sure anymore.

"You didn't need to come here—not for respect or anything else," Cross told her, sighing as he cracked his knuckles and leaned back into the booth. "The contract with The League is void. You're free to do what you want without my input, and honestly, I expect you to do just that."

Well, then …

"I am," she replied softly.

"Then, you're lying. *Again.* Like that night in the office on your birthday. You didn't come here for the respect of the matter because I'm sure nothing I have said is anything you didn't already know. Or suspect, either way. What are you lying about now?"

Penny swallowed hard, hating how he was right. "I'm trying to figure out something."

"What?"

"What comes after, I guess. If there is one for me. I've been thinking about it. I have a lot of time to do that sort of thing lately. Apparently, they just kept me busy to keep me from thinking ... not because I was doing what everyone else wouldn't."

Cross considered her with that hard stare of his. The silence between them dragged on until she thought maybe it would be better to just turn around and leave. "That depends, Penny."

"On what?"

"When the *after* is." He lifted one shoulder, the blazer he wore custom fit to his tall form while the gold cufflinks caught the lights overhead when he waved an arm. "Because as soon as you do something irreversible that would hurt The League, they're going to answer with an equal action. It's inevitable. And you've made things easy—the cleanup, I mean—with the bounty. Can't say I've ever heard of someone signing their own death warrant in such a way."

The longer she stared at the man who had only been a part of her life for the last few years from a distance, the more she thought about the last time they had truly *talked.* Not the usual orders in a file, a new job discussed over a conference call, or a message passed between her handlers and delivered to her. They were never ... a team.

It wasn't like that.

"I keep thinking back to when I was that terrified eighteen-year-old girl asking you to help me in that office," Penny said, "and everything felt so hopeless. You were the only person that had a solution to my problem, but it didn't get better."

"The hopelessness?"

"Yeah."

"And the solution wasn't what I expected it to be, either. It did change everything for me, though."

"For the better?" he asked.

Well ... *look at me,* she thought. Was it better?

"That's yet to be determined," Penny murmured in reply as she turned on her heel to leave, saying, "Thank you for seeing me tonight."

"Penny," Cross called at her back.

She hesitated. "What?"

"I hear there's an important event coming up for Senator Tracey—an official engagement dinner to Allegra Hatheway."

Her throat tightened with flaring anger that rose up from the pits of her empty belly. Even eating lately was an added chore. "It's nothing."

"*Lies.* It's the first—maybe only—opening you'll have to kill her. They know it, too. The League, The Elite. They'll be expecting you there. Is that a risk you're going to take?"

"What choice do I have?"

Even if it might kill her.

"Good luck," Cross said.

Penny headed down the stairs, saying to herself, "I don't need luck—I'm still trying to find hope."

• • •

The roof of the office building currently undergoing construction in its underground garage was twenty stories high. With lax security and a clear view of the Manhattan restaurant situated diagonally from the office building where Penny worked fast behind the shelter of an air conditioning system.

One piece at a time, her rifle came together under her skilled hands. The sniper would allow her miles of vision, but she only needed the block of distance between her roof and the front of the restaurant where her mother would soon be arriving alongside her senator fiancé.

The rattling of the air conditioning system was loud in her ear. Darkness coated her every movement, only the glow of lights from nearby buildings and a single security light somewhere at her back giving her any visibility to work.

Nothing she couldn't handle.

Nothing she hadn't done before.

She wouldn't usually pick a spot like this to work. Beyond the difficulties the roof provided to her plan, the noise was distracting. No sniper with any choice in the matter would willingly choose to take long-distance shots through crosswinds while an air conditioner roared beside them. It was made for disaster.

A missed shot.

It was also perfect for Penny.

Or rather, perfect for what she needed. The large metal shades on the system kept her hidden from view of anyone who might be on a higher, nearby roof watching for her. The roof of the office building itself, despite the crosswinds, allowed her a perfect view directly inside the front of the restaurant through the windows, a good portion of the road, and the entrance of the business.

It couldn't *get* better.

With only the barrel of her rifle sticking out on the side of the roof, Penny laid flat to the cement and came eye-level with the scope on her gun. The case lay open beside her, waiting and ready for her to dismantle and pack up the weapon as quickly as she arrived to unpack it.

The butt rested comfortably against her shoulder as she moved the sights to scan the road and entrance of the restaurant. Cars were already arriving, dropping off the only people who would have access to the business for the evening. Guests of the engagement party between Senator Gilles Tracey and Allegra Hatheway.

Penny checked the windows, too, and the people inside. Some faces she recognized, but that was only from old family ties. She wasn't late—or too early. History and the expectations of people like her mother's family told her that some shit never changed. The party might have started ten minutes ago, but the guests of the hour were never late. Everyone else was always early.

Penny didn't mind waiting.

Soon, a black car with a familiar flag attached to the front and rear of the vehicle pulled up to the entrance of the restaurant. Even if Penny hadn't noticed the political flags, the security that quickly moved from the entrance of the business to the sidewalk where they could open the rear doors of the car said more than enough. Another black car pulled up right behind, suits stepping out from every angle just to surround the town car with legs spread shoulder-width apart and hands folded at their backs.

She didn't care about them.

Gilles Tracey stepped out of the car first—then, Allegra. Wearing a royal blue gown that matched the color of her soon-to-be husband's vest and tie. The wind in the city streets had the skirt of the gown billowing around the two as they shared words, and the security stepped further back with neutral expressions.

At least *they* were neutral.

Allegra and Gilles were anything but. The man with gray at his temples whispered something Allegra's way, his narrowed gaze and shake of his head saying more than what Penny could understand through the sights of her scope.

The man wasn't happy.

Allegra tried to *soothe* … like she did.

It didn't work.

Body language spoke volumes—theirs was screaming. *Yeah*, Penny bet it was hard to sleep next to Allegra lately what with all the trouble Penny had caused for her mother and the senator. She couldn't say she was sorry for it.

The only problem?

Penny didn't have a clear shot.

But she might if only the senator would just mo—

"If you shoot," she heard a dark, but familiar, voice say from somewhere behind her, "then anyone looking for you within a five-block radius will know exactly where you are. This building is twenty stories high—you'll never make it down before someone is here."

Penny had been holding her breath. The air slipped out with a name as her shoulders sagged, "Luca."

She didn't look away from the scope—didn't know where he was except behind her. She didn't take her finger off the trigger, either.

"Let's be real, they're all here—anyone wanting to claim the bounty, people from The League … *definitely* protection for Allegra. You've made it entirely possible for them to connect the dots. Why wouldn't they be here? You'll have, at most, two minutes. Can you do this in two minutes, babe?"

God.

She still didn't move even as she asked Luca, "How did you find me?"

10.

"HOW did you find me?"

Luca drew in the cold whisper of the wind with his next breath, wishing for even a second that he could remember what it felt like to be sane again. Penny's question hung in the air between them, although from his vantage point where he had exited onto the roof through a hatched door, he could see her body flattened against the roof. He imagined he didn't have the same vantage point as her, though, seeing as how she hadn't looked away from the scope on the rather impressive rifle for even a blink in time.

Who was she seeing?

Someone driving on the street? A passerby on the sidewalk? Her *target?* Allegra?

Luca couldn't help but wonder if he was too late—it always felt like he arrived seconds after the big bang at every fucking point in his life.

"Well?" he heard her ask. "How?"

The question seemed simple. It wasn't.

"Details aren't really important," he tried to say.

Hoping she took the deflection. She didn't.

"But they always are. Especially in your business," she tacked on for good measure. As if he needed the goddamn reminder.

Details were what got him here in the first place.

He'd been awake for going on forty-two hours. All it took was a single, early-morning phone call from his godfather. Cross confirmed what Luca already believed—Penny was going to take her chance of making a hit on Allegra at the woman's official engagement dinner in Manhattan. Luca suddenly found himself in the heart of a city pouring over every square inch of a six-block radius that he could because …

Shit, she had to be there. That's where she was *going to be.*

No one could tell Luca that in all her years of training as an assassin that Penny would leave things to chance. She was exactly the type to stand out in a crowd—dangerous for her considering the current circumstances of a bounty on her head—so he expected he would have to find her in the shadows.

But the days turned into hours. And then minutes.

Luca should have been used to chasing ghosts by now, but it didn't get easier. For whatever reason, the universe had decided to bless him with putting him in the right place at the right time that morning as he watched

Penny scout the office building with several floors currently undergoing construction.

She was just there. He thought he'd hallucinated.

But no.

"In most cases," he said, staying back behind the shadowed line that the hatch door afforded him. A three- or four-foot space on the roof separated him and Penny—a stream of yellow light illuminating the nothingness between them from the security light overhead. He doubted anyone could see her from the position she rested under the metal hood of the air conditioning unit, though. "But not for you. See, when I treated you like anything—anyone else—that I was tasked with finding, it always led me nowhere. You were never the same. You're not like other people ... or things. How can I expect you to act like it?"

She made different choices. Her reasoning came from a different place. It couldn't be the same.

He watched Penny's back rise with a deep breath that he had to wonder was meant to steady her when she said, "If I ask you to leave—"

"I won't."

"You have to."

She still hadn't looked away from the scope. That crosswind came in strong with the next gust, and Penny cussed as her elbow tucked back along her side, telling him she had been preparing for a shot.

"I can't fucking *get it*," she muttered.

He still had a chance to make her think clearly. It was one last thread for him to grasp on and use because the rest of him felt battered like an old flag from the winds of chaos that this woman could create.

"It's a big night—you know this is a stupid fucking move," Luca told Penny. While the black fabric of her cropped tank top and cargo pants melted into the shadows around her, he could still see the way she tensed at the truth. "So you make a clean kill but then what—you spend the next six blocks in a gunfight with every person that's hunting you.. There's got to be a better way, Penny."

"She can't keep living."

That was it.

That was all she said.

And God knew he understood ...

Penny was born into privilege. She had every reason to *succeed*. Except the people meant to love her had been the same people who hurt her in ways no one would ever truly comprehend. There was no innocence—no chance to *be* innocent. No gray when the world had to be so very black and white for her. She couldn't be normal when they had broken her first, and then someone else had to go and make her the *exceptional*.

Only to tell her she couldn't be that, either.

An exceptional lie.

He wondered if her entire life felt like it had led up to this moment. If so, then yes, he understood perfectly well why she wanted to take her chance tonight. Despite the risks, he might even do the same.

He simply didn't think she had to.

"Penny—"

"She can't keep being *free*," Penny snarled from the ground.

"But you could do this in a better way."

He dared to take a step forward, but that was the wrong move. The noise of his sneakers scuffing the roof had Penny jerking away from the rifle. She moved like lightning, sliding gracefully to her feet and darting through and beyond the stream of light to push him back toward the stairwell leading inward from the hatched door.

"Stay out of the light," she told him.

Not *go*.

Not *leave me alone*.

Not even *this is my business*.

All of which he would have understood and even respected. Instead, she told him to stay out of the light, and he knew why. Anyone higher might see them—*her*. Him. He locked stares with her, desperate to find what she had left behind there. That *thing* growing between them. He was sure he found it in her wide blue orbs that reflected fear when her hand hit his chest again and she hissed, "Goddammit—stay out of the light, Luca."

"Penny—"

"I didn't have a clear shot."

That was all she said before she turned away, ready to head back for her rifle. The festering anger and panic that had accompanied him from the moment he realized she had left him behind in Nevada finally came rushing to the surface when she dared to walk away from him at that moment.

"Don't fucking walk away from me again."

His hand stuck out hand, finding the back of her neck in a tight grasp that had Penny gasping when he yanked her back to him. She spun around under his handling, and he was already closing the distance between them. His mouth crushed to hers, and the kiss that consumed them both reminded him of drowning. He knew he needed to breathe, that he should try to come up for air. Except he didn't want to when he could taste her on his tongue, and the very heat of her mouth proved she was *alive*.

The kiss ached. Every stroke of their lips came rougher than the last. His chest took the pummeling from his racing heart in stride, but he couldn't say the same for his nerves.

Or his soul.

That was all hers anyway.

His hand loosened at the nape of Penny's neck, but not enough that she could move away from him when he murmured against her lips, "If you do end it here, then I'm here to help you do it. No matter what. You're not alone. You don't have to be alone—*I'm here*. Let me be here, Penny."

Because didn't she know?

He'd never wanted to stop her.

Only help.

11.

IT was Luca's eyes that could kill Penny. Those green-blue orbs of his that always seemed to stare right *at* her, landing on her with a heaviness that she could feel. No one ever looked at her the way he did. They either looked through her, overlooked her, or tried to find something they could change.

But not him.

Not her Luca.

Because he was.

Hers.

She just wasn't sure if he knew it—it's why he was one of the last things she felt like she had to worry about while she finished her business. Before this, he had been her friend, and then for years he had been a piece of her past that just wouldn't let go. He had become her temptation, too. She didn't doubt that after this, he would still be hers in some way.

They could get back to it.

Maybe.

Except he kept coming back. Finding her at all the wrong times. *Fucking me up*, she thought.

His intense stare still hadn't let go of hers when she dared to ask him, "Why do you keep trying to save me? Haven't you figured out that I don't exactly *need* saving? I'm not the damsel here—I'm not even sure there's a hero."

If anything, she was one of the villains. Just in a different way.

Luca's mouth twitched upward in the corner, almost like he might *smirk*. "I never tried to save you—that was everybody else's job. I only ever wanted to help."

Penny pulled in a shuddering breath that ached. "One might say leaving is a good indication that I don't want help, Luca."

"It's not that you don't want my help—you think you don't need it. There's a difference, Penny."

She could still taste him on her lips. Never had a man grabbed her so roughly at the back of her neck without the intention of doing her body some kind of harm … except for him. He'd kissed her like his life depended on it, and for a second, she was sure hers *had*. The imprint of his mouth would linger on hers for days, she was sure.

But it was wonderful.

And horrible, too.

Penny inched backward, only a slice of her pinky finger sliding into the stream of illuminated color from the security light overhead. Luca didn't let her move very far before his fingers flexed at her nape and he murmured, "I know you went back—*home*, I mean. And little Cross, well you promised him you were going to try to go back, right? Are you still trying or did you lie to him?"

Low blow.

So fucking low it hurt.

Penny's chin quivered with the emotions that she tried to clench between her teeth. It didn't work. She was all too aware that every second she was away from her gun was one that was lost forever. She would never get it back.

Not that it mattered.

It was already too late.

"You don't get to do that," she told him, wishing so badly that her fingers didn't itch with the desire to stroke the lines of his face with her fingertips. Carved from stone and handed to her like God had taken time on this man just for her … Luca didn't know the power he possessed over Penny. A part of her hoped he never would. "You don't get to tell me you're not going to stop me, but in the next breath try to manipulate me into—"

"Actually, I'm just thinking like you. Because I had to do that for a while to figure out what I missed here. I think I went insane for a little bit. It's hard to be the monster you must see in the mirror when you've always been just human, sweetheart."

Why?

Why did he have to do that?

She was the reflection of her mother. She could have *been* Allegra had she just … been worthy, right? All of that left her cold and *sick*.

"I missed the mark," she whispered. "Didn't have a clear shot."

Luca swallowed hard. "I'm sorry."

"Someone is still going to die tonight."

"But not like this," he returned.

No.

Because while he had been right about a lot of things, he was also wrong about one. She would have taken the chance to kill Allegra from the roof even if the cost was her life. It would have been worth it.

The only thing Penny cared to ask in that moment was, "What are you driving?"

His answer made her smile.

"An old favorite I keep in storage just for city driving when I need it— my Ducati."

Perfect.

• • •

The only sound in the dark alley was the constant *drip-drip-drip* of water falling from the eaves of two buildings. Penny wasn't opposed to rain on a job—sometimes, it even worked in her favor when the danger didn't scare her in the first place. The noise helped to muffle Luca's question that came behind the black visor of his helmet.

He only had one.

She made him wear it.

Penny should be seen, anyway.

"How do you want me to do—"

"Just drive," she told him.

Staring at her through the visor from over his shoulder, she wondered if he was looking at the gun in her hand while she worked the silencer into the barrel, or *her*. Calm and focused, gaze on her work as she spoke softly. Unfeeling about what might happen next.

It's who she was.

Now.

"Just drive, don't look anywhere but the street ahead of you—drive *fast*," she said.

"Who are you going for?"

"Anybody. A face I recognize. My mother if I get the chance through the windows but that's unlikely. I don't *care*. She'll know I was here."

"Are you—"

Before he could even finish his question, Penny reached over and poked the tip of her finger against Luca's visor. She couldn't see his face through the dark tint, but she would have given *anything* to in that moment. Her left arm, even.

"Help me and drive, Luca."

Maybe there was a hint of a smirk in his tone when he replied, "Drive—got it, babe."

It was the second time he called her that tonight.

She was starting to like it.

Sticking the gun into the holster at her chest, Penny used a bandana that had been tied to the handlebars to wrap up her hair as Luca's Ducati Superbike roared to life. Matte black like his helmet, the beast would do just fine for what she had planned. It moved like lightning but with the gracefulness of shadows.

What more could she ask for?

The first jerk of the bike sent Penny leaning in close to Luca. She didn't need to look up to see where they were—she had tracked these streets and alleys—even the buildings—from the moment she knew where Allegra would be having her engagement party in the city.

She also didn't need to see to know what was happening. From the road of the bike and the pressure that sent her body leaning back a bit said when Luca was speeding up—probably to miss the set of lights that might possibly be turning yellow. They couldn't stop. Not once they left the alley.

The bike leaned hard to the right when they took the turn at the lights while Penny leaned with Luca, one hand wrapped tight around his waist while her other grasped firmly to the butt of the gun inside the holster at her chest. Tucked down like she was, someone might not even notice her on the back of the bike until they passed.

It all worked.

But then she counted the seconds when the bike roared and darted forward with more speed—*one, two, and then three* ... Penny leaned up from her tightly tucked position, already pulling the gun from the holster as the Ducati growled past the restaurant on the other side of the street. She aimed the gun, gaze already scanning as the black bandana pulled away from her hair in the wind.

It was better than she ever imagined.

Her grandfather had just arrived.

It took all of a second.

Less, even.

The League would never forgive her for what she had done to them, but at least they trained her to be one hell of a shot on the back of a moving vehicle.

Charles Hatheway saw her—their gazes locked as the bike passed—when she pulled the trigger. She didn't get to see it hit the intended target before they had already gone by, but she heard the screams.

Those were beautiful.

12.

Luca

"IS it appropriate for me to say a small prayer?"

Penny shot Luca a look from where she stood behind his beloved Ducati. He didn't get to drive the machine nearly enough for his tastes. He'd spent a crazy amount of money for the bike and *on it* to get it customized just the way he liked. The damn thing even had its own storage unit in the city because he absolutely refused to drive it in the winter, or on any road that wasn't pristine.

He loved the bike.

If he had a baby, it was it.

"Thought we agreed getting rid of it was the only option?" Penny asked.

Luca sighed, ghosting his hands over the curves of the matte black beast. From the handlebars, down the seat, and even over the rear flare. "I'll see you again soon," he told the bike.

That was a lie.

Soon, it would be at the bottom of the river.

"You can always buy another," Penny said with more care to her tone. He didn't know if it was a genuine concern for his feelings or just her patronizing him, though. It could have gone either way. *Damn woman.*

She also wasn't wrong.

"Fuck it," Luca muttered.

Grabbing the back of the seat in one hand and the left handlebar with his other, Luca pushed the bike to the end of the dock. There was never much movement at the shipping docks this time of night. The shift change made sure of that, and he was grateful because it worked in their favor when they needed to make the bike disappear. He was sure there were probably a few dozen people scouting for a matte black Ducati Superbike with two possible drivers. Letting them find the machine would only connect him to the shooting.

The Ducati hit the water with a plop and a splash. Luca watched it sink from up above before he bent down to grab the helmet he'd tossed on the dock earlier. With a few larger rocks in the bottom of the helmet, he expected it to sink.

Another item he could replace. Like the bike, too. But goddammit, it still hurt like hell to watch the bike disappear under the depths of the water while the helmet bobbed and struggled to fall beneath the surface as well.

Penny was soon at Luca's side to survey the scene down below as well. Without warning, she reached beneath the jacket he'd given her after they arrived at the docks. She didn't say she was cold, but he saw her shiver and that shit wasn't okay. Not when he had a perfectly fine leather jacket that she could use.

The white strands of her hair fell over the shoulder of his jacket as she stretched her arm toward the water. With two well-aimed shots of her gun to the helmet, it finally sunk below the water with a bubbled *glub-glub,* and that was it. A sad little goodbye, really.

The night was almost over.

"You didn't have to do *that,*" Luca told her.

Penny's right eyebrow quirked up when she replied dryly, "Might as well use the other bullets for something useful."

Ouch.

He said nothing when she dropped down to sit at the edge of the dock. Instead, he moved to stand behind her so that at the very least, he was there if she needed him. For anything.

"It's not over," she told him.

"Not yet," he agreed. "Now we go back to the drawing board and figure out where we go from her."

Down below, her head bobbed with a nod. He couldn't help but notice how she didn't correct his use of *we* when it came to their next plan. Hell, wasn't that a battle won in itself? He sure as fuck thought so.

As the silence stretched on, another question nagged at Luca. It would be in his best interest to stay quiet and *not* ask it, but he wasn't the type. For one. But for two … he hated to think Penny might be hurting in that moment because of what she had done—in some way—and he wasn't helping her.

Fuck him for having a heart.

Right?

She probably didn't want him to ask anything at all. Silence and running were her best friends, after all. He couldn't help himself, though.

"Did you get a hit back at the restaurant?"

Penny's shoulders stiffened, but otherwise, she didn't move on the dock below him. "I did—and while it wasn't Allegra, it was about as good as her."

"Who?"

She'd been able to recognize them as they passed? Shit, he'd been breaking seventy at that point. After they'd gone by entirely, he gunned it further and brought the front tire up from the road. At least by then, Penny had been back to holding onto him. God knew they didn't need to end up rolling across pavement at that point.

"Penny?" Luca asked when a minute passed without a reply. "Who was it?"

Her head tipped down, and he hated that he couldn't see her face to understand *why*. Her next words helped a bit with it. "My grandfather, Charles. He would need to go eventually—had the original plans moved forward, he was next on the list. Essentially anyone else was useless and easy kills. They could send teams for them. It would have left me with only Allegra and ... she would have had to know it was me."

"Coming for her," Luca supplied.

Penny exhaled harshly. "Well, she does know. At any rate, it works."

Then, Luca had another thought. Fuck his thoughts lately, too, because they were getting him in more trouble than they were worth. So was his damn life.

"Did your grandfather abus—"

"No," she interjected before he could ask more. "He had a revolving door of children at his disposal—he was the gatekeeper. They would give him anything to get what they wanted. Allegra, though ... that was different. She was always jealous whenever he paid me any kind of attention. I look so much like her and back then, it was worse. It was bad all over."

"How so?"

"You don't want to know, Luca. It's all ... rotten."

A chill settled deep in Luca's veins, but he didn't show it. Everything about Penny's history was uncomfortable. To deal with, to talk about, or even *think* inside the privacy of his own mind. He couldn't imagine what it must be like to actually *be* her.

"And I just hate her," Penny added. "In the end, that's where I settle it. I hate her."

Well ...

He understood that.

Too well.

"We should go," he murmured.

He hated to do it. Penny seemed content in her quiet stillness on the dock. With her legs hanging over the edge, swishing to and fro, she didn't seem ready to move. Not that it mattered; they didn't have a choice.

"Better not linger," Luca added. "We wouldn't want to be noticed when I'm sure every hound in this city is out sniffing for you."

Penny dared to glance over her shoulder, her blue gaze glittering up at him when she asked, "Literally or figuratively?"

"Well," he considered, "maybe a bit of both."

Her laughter was the best sound in the world, but especially because he hadn't been expecting it in the first place. Before he could think better of it, Luca placed his outstretched hand down for Penny to take. Palm up, he left it open.

She could take his help—even if it was only to get up—should she want to. Or, his hand could be there for her to take when she stood up without his help.

Luca grinned when she pulled on his hand to steady herself to her feet. The windswept mess of her hair still managed to look good, especially with that smile stretching over her pretty face. Then, her hand squeezed his when she asked, "He told you I came back—little Cross, I mean?"

"Yeah, he did."

"Did he tell anyone—"

"You mean like his parents because you could have put him in serious danger just by being anywhere *near* him?"

Penny's stare narrowed. "I didn't mean for him to see me in the first place. He was just ... *there*. And then I couldn't even trick or lie to him because he's—"

"Way too smart for that."

"Kind of amazing, actually."

Luca smirked. "Some people call him strange."

"Yeah, well, fuck those people."

He chuckled.

Right.

Fuck those people.

"But I didn't lie to him," Penny whispered, locking stares with Luca when she inched closer. "I *do* want to go back."

"I know. That's why I'm here. We all want that."

"Even you."

"Especially me."

He dared her to ask why.

He wanted to tell her.

"If you'll let me," he added quieter.

Instead of asking the question he wanted her to, Penny asked, "But what does that even mean?"

"Stop running. You don't do this alone. It means I'm here."

"So—"

Luca yanked her closer using their still-connected hands until they were chest to chest and eye to eye. "What's the plan, Penny?"

He really only wanted one thing.

Right then, anyway.

She gave it to him when her plush, pink lips pressed against his without warning. And just like that, Luca couldn't breathe all over again. His chest tightened with every dance of her lips across his, and then when her tongue darted into his mouth for a taste, he swore the world tilted. Just a little. Just *enough*.

He wanted to touch her.

Gets his hands all over her.

He wanted her safe.

He just wanted her.

Luca didn't care what the plan was—not as long as they did it together.

• • •

"Thank you, Mrs. Titchens. Enjoy your stay for the evening—and your husband. I hope you can get a refund at the other hotel for the cancellations."

Penny beamed at the woman behind the desk. "Me, too. Especially since they lost our stuff. How do you do that in a hotel, anyway?"

Sabrina, according to her nametag, only shrugged when she replied, "Sometimes, things just happen. I was happy to figure something out for you here instead. It all worked out in the end."

Right, Luca thought.

By *worked out* the woman meant she had allowed Luca and Penny to rent a room in the hotel for the night—but likely more—all based on a lie. Because they didn't have identification, at least he didn't have a fake ID, and Penny hadn't carried anything on her for the night except what she absolutely needed to. He had twenty-five hundred dollars in hundreds inside his wallet, and money spoke louder than any words they could say, anyway.

Penny made up the lie.

They got the room.

"And here is your keycard—have a good night!"

Penny took the sleek, silver card from the short, redhead with another smile. "Thank you."

Luca scanned the front entrance of the hotel, slightly uncomfortable with the amount of glass that allowed him a decent view of the street outside. They were far enough inside the business that even if someone did recognize them, they would probably need a second look. He would have preferred a hotel with a less open reception, but maybe that was Penny's point.

She didn't actually *hide.* Everyone was looking for her where she couldn't be found.

"Mr. Titchens?"

Luca's distraction cost him the sight of Penny heading for the elevator. The receptionist gave him a smile—probably thinking he was tired and over the entire day after the tale Penny spun for the woman—and then nodded after the piece of art currently looking back over her shoulder at him. The wavy, textured length of her white-blonde hair fell down to her mid-back, swaying just over the spot where he knew she had two dimples above the curve of her backside. But her ass was still quite a sight covered in tight, black cargo pants.

It wasn't even the time.

He had better—far more important—things to focus on other than how hard he could get just watching Penny walk away from him. Except he couldn't think about anything else but that because Luca was *fucked*.

Penny winked and tilted her chin in a silent demand for him to follow. He shook his head with a chuckle, not even bothered by the fact she watched him check her out without shame. Why should he be? *Look at her.*

She was still there.

Still *real.*

Things were already looking up.

13.

LUCA wasn't a loud man—never had been—and it was one of the things Penny liked about him the most. He was such a presence without actually making himself *present*. He didn't fill the silence when someone else was quiet. She couldn't even remember a time when he had tried to take center stage ahead of anyone in his life.

He reminded her of a pillar. Fortitude in the storm. Strength under pressure. Everything that she was sure he didn't even realize about himself. Because why would he—the man was too busy trying to make the rest of the world happy instead of taking care of himself.

She was part of that, too.

Penny knew it.

She also knew Luca would never tell her that, so when he was quiet in the elevator ride up to the room she had managed to snag for the night, his presence felt heavier to her. Not for any particular reason that she could pinpoint; his face gave nothing away when those shadowy green-blue eyes of his darted her way.

He just ... *was*.

Maybe he *did* want to fill the silence. She could feel the way his gaze crawled over her as the elevator moved higher—beyond the third floor. A slow trek upward. She decided to say something for Luca. Or perhaps she just couldn't take the quietness anymore.

"You can't go back to your apartment," she said, wishing her voice had more strength to it and less ... *quiver*. Luca's stare jumped from the spot where it had been lingering on the column of her neck to meet hers. "It's not safe. Especially if someone connects you to me tonight and—"

"I get it."

Penny nodded once. If he didn't want to argue about it, then she was grateful. "Thanks. It'll still be there when this is over."

The hint of a smirk teased his features when he asked, "But what does that even mean—when this is over? What's *over*, Penny?"

She really wished there was an answer. At least, one that would satisfy him.

But ... "I don't know. But it will be over. Someday."

It had to be.

She was kind of banking on that now.

The headiness of her sadness filled up Penny's chest without warning. She didn't want to be sad—couldn't afford an emotion with consequences that had always left her hurt and bleeding in the past. In one way or another.

"*Hey*," she heard him say.

He was still watching her. Probably wouldn't let her out of his sight, she knew. Strangely, she was okay with that.

She thought he had something to tell her—like he was reading her mind—but instead, his hand reached for hers. It started with nothing more than the graze of his pinky against hers. Just the tip, and then the side of the digit brushing hers softly. It took nothing for her to slide her palm in alongside his. Their fingers wove tight, and she watched how well his hand fit with hers.

Still silent, he was the pillar.

There was only one thing she thought about in that moment—one she really wanted. It certainly wasn't the time, and she had too many other things to focus on except getting Luca Puzza closer to her, but she didn't care.

Not one bit.

Penny only needed to tug gently on Luca's hand to make him close the space between them, but there was nothing gentle about his approach. She didn't mind it at all when he crowded her and backed her hard into the elevator wall. His hand stayed tangled with hers while his other hand came up to flatten against her throat. That tempting mouth of his, never hesitating, meet hers in a kiss that had her heart thumping viciously for more.

His kiss was hungry.

Mouth, and teeth, and tongue.

His palm at her throat flexed when the elevator dared to jump before coming to a stop. Not that it separated the two of them. The weight of him was substantial, keeping Penny pinned in place to melt against a man she didn't mind letting haunt her dreams.

He smelled like leather and man—like the city and smoke and *them*. Every strike of his tongue against hers took away another breath from her lungs until the organ ached for any kind of relief.

Between kisses and hard exhales, she managed to whisper, "We're on our floor, and—"

Luca pulled away all at once, but he dragged her with him, yanking her between the closing elevator doors in the very last second. All she saw was him looking back at her while they headed down the hall.

That was perfect.

He was all she wanted to see, anyway.

• • •

Penny didn't really remember how they made their way into the shower, but the hot water pelted at her chest while Luca's hands did wonderful things to her thighs. His deft fingers worked into knots she didn't even realize had been keeping her muscles tight until he got every single one of them out. Her little moans of relief drowned in the waterfall spray of water overhead.

"Good?"

Penny smiled, her eyes still closed when she felt his hands dance lower to her calves. "Better."

"How many miles have you clocked?"

On her feet?

In the past week, too many. More than she ever would again. It was just faster to walk to get where she wanted to go—the subway did the major distance, but even still, she didn't regret investing in boots for work that didn't do a number on her feet.

"A lot," she settled on saying.

Luca hummed a dark and delicious sound that had Penny opening her eyes. He was quite a sight kneeled down in front of her, naked, back wet with water droplets and skin pebbled from the cold air. He wasn't under the spray like she was, not that he seemed to mind. The man was content *doing* not *being*.

She would rather do something for him.

"Come here," Penny said, reaching for him through the water and foggy space. He didn't hesitate to stand, never questioning *her*. Like everything else going on, too. He was just there—letting her be. As he stood, leaning in and unbothered by the spray of hot water, she mouthed the words, *"Kiss me."*

And he did.

Again.

Like in the elevator.

Or how he devoured her the second they were hidden within the privacy of the hotel room. There wasn't much to look at in there but each other, anyway. If for the moment, she couldn't do anything to further what was happening outside these walls, then she wanted to do nothing at all with Luca.

If nothing meant doing him.

Of course.

But this time when he kissed her, she let him take his taste of her mouth while her hands dipped lower between them. One tightened around the base of his semi-hard shaft, stroking him from base to tip before swiping the tip of her thumb over the head of his cock. He shuddered, his teeth catching her bottom lip when she dared to cup and stroke his balls with her other hand at the same time.

"*Fuck*," he hissed.

His pupils blew wide when their kiss slowed because her hands picked up the pace. Tugging faster, tightening with a twist of her wrist, and then stroking his balls while her tongue teased the seam of his lips, too.

She had to ask, "Does anyone ever take care of *you?*"

Luca blinked.

He didn't answer.

She really didn't need him to.

Her name came out of his mouth like someone had slammed a fist against his chest when he came. Spilling sticky cum on her fingers that the water washed away.

Mostly.

She kneeled down to lick the rest off while he watched.

• • •

"I have to leave in the morning," Penny said, although it was the last thing she wanted to do. She didn't want to interrupt the quiet stillness she and Luca had found tangled naked in bed. They could have closed the blinds but instead, they watched the dark sky stretch on for hours.

What was sleep?

Luca's arms tightened around Penny's middle. She even felt the twitch of his jaw when his stubble scraped tantalizingly against her scarred stomach. He never shied away from the history she had cut into her skin. In fact, the canvas of her skin, from the soft spots behind her knees to the one that made her shiver at the back of her neck became his personal map to do with what he wanted. She'd never enjoyed being studied more.

"I'll go with—"

"Better not," she said, meeting his gaze when he lifted his head from her stomach. "I have to grab some things from a shitty motel. Less foot travel from both of us is best right now. I'll be back. Maybe before you wake up."

Luca arched a brow.

He didn't believe her.

"Are you going to run again?" he asked.

She should have expected that. Hell, he was owed it.

"I'll be *back*," she said.

As good as a promise.

And she wouldn't argue.

If people hadn't figured it out yet, Penny was going to do whatever she wanted and needed to do whether someone else wanted her to do it or not. It would happen. They could get in line, or move out of the way.

She adored Luca.

But he wasn't an exception.

"Come back," he murmured.

"I said I would."

"And still—"

"I *will*."

The sharpness of her words sent him rising up to hover above her. He was quite a sight—every hard line of his muscles from the ropes that made up his arms to the bands of his shoulders, and even the hard expanse of his chest. If living artwork was a thing, then Luca was surely it.

A drug.

Made just for her.

She wanted another hit.

As quickly as the two had melted into silence to watch the darkness creep through the skies, they as easily moved back into something carnal. All it took was the widening of her thighs when he pressed in between her, and the way she dragged her fingernails from his chest down to his stomach and over his sides.

He got himself hard by kissing her while she rubbed against him. She found paradise when he filled her full, the sting of being stretched open again that night too delicious not to share. Her nails bit into his skin to give it back just as much.

He said nothing.

No dark words.

No dirty promises.

Not while he watched and fucked her. He just took in everything she gave. Each little sound. How her air started to catch when his pace came in with fast, long relentless strokes. His hands tightened to her small waist, holding tight enough to hurt while her fingers locked around his wrists.

She came hard like that.

She bet he still didn't believe her, though. He wouldn't say it—but he was hurt. Because she left him. She didn't give him a reason not to be.

Either way ...

Penny would come back.

• • •

"Actually, she just walked through the door, Naz," Luca said as the hotel's door clicked shut under Penny's hand.

She hadn't expected to sleep beyond nine—she blamed Luca for that—so the trip to the motel took longer than she expected. With the sun crawling high in the sky, it was already well past noon. At least, Luca didn't seem surprised that she was back.

Maybe he had believed her.

She didn't expect to get back and find him on the phone with Nazio, though. She didn't know whether to deal with that first, or the fact that the small nineteen-inch flatscreen television was turned on showcasing a news reporter discussing her mother.

Allegra's face—in a photograph from her wedding to Penny's father— stayed plastered in the top, left-hand corner of the screen as the woman behind the glass desk spoke.

"Thousands of images of Allegra Dunsworth's estranged—and currently *missing*—daughter, Penny Dunsworth, have surfaced all over the internet. What appeared as a file dump of child pornography on the dark web quickly made its way to the public interwebs on chat forums. It was a quick leap from there to being widely shared across social media platforms as people connected—"

"Shut it off," Penny said, air stinging in her chest.

She knew it was going to hurt. She knew it would be bad. Yet. Penny hadn't been ready.

Luca didn't say anything, simply reached for the small remote to point at the television. It took a press of one button for the screen to blank out entirely. Immediately, she felt better. The anxiety ebbed away, but it was a false sense of security. Everything was still *out* there. She couldn't take that back.

Ever.

Luca muttered something to the man on the phone. A quick, "Yeah, all right." Then, he set it down on the small table beside the loveseat at the foot of the bed. She thought he hung it up, but apparently, he just put it on speakerphone.

"She there?" Naz asked.

Penny swallowed hard, giving Luca a look.

He only shrugged back.

Damn.

"I'm here," she said.

Naz took a second.

And then another.

"You dumped the files?"

Penny glanced Luca's way, but he watched the dark screen of the television like he couldn't get the image out of his head of the reporter discussing the thousands of files—she knew it was horrifying. The images and videos of her abuse ranged from simple scenes of grooming to totally debasing acts.

Had he seen some?

It was an unfortunate by-product of her choice. Innocent people would have to be affected—and subjected—to the dark reality in the world. She was sorry for that. Regret was a whole other matter entirely.

"I had someone else dump the files," Penny told Naz. "Yes."

Had he wanted a different answer?

Penny didn't care to ask.

"I've essentially plastered Allegra's history and the things she would rather hide where everyone can see," Penny said. "I've ruined any chance of her soon-to-be husband continuing his political career beyond what he has. I'm sure the consensus among his team is no comment, and I assume Allegra's side of things will be the same. Let them lick their wounds while they plan a funeral for her father. It gives me some time to get ahead."

Luca let out a hard breath. "*Well ...*"

"Yeah," Naz muttered in reply on the phone.

Penny never said this would be easy.

None of it.

"We miss you, Penny," Naz said suddenly. "I hope you know that."

Luca gave her a small smile. She couldn't help but do the same back when she replied to the man on the phone, "I know, and when this is all over ..."

She stopped herself from saying more.

Naz chuckled, saying, "Yeah, when this is all over."

Things would be different.

She needed that.

14.

PENNY dropped a single duffle bag to the couch when the call clicked off with Naz. Luca dipped his chin in the direction of the bag, asking, "Did you get everything you needed?"

"Well, I didn't bring anything I don't need."

Smartass.

He liked it, though.

Penny shrugged and ripped open the zipper on the bag to show him what was inside. Other than the pack for the dismantled sniper rifle she'd been using the night before, she hadn't been traveling with more. He gave the items at the top of the bag a cursory glance; it wasn't anything particularly interesting and everything that he expected.

Bands of cash.

Clothes.

Knives.

He suspected there were probably a couple of guns at the bottom, and whatever else Penny might need to get by.

"I had more," she said, pulling the zipper closed again, "just in case. But I don't really need it. Dumped it on the way back here."

"As long as you're satisfied."

She gave him a second look.

Fuck.

Maybe Luca hadn't tempered his tone enough to hide the anxious note lingering in his words.

"You didn't think I would come back," she said.

Luca sighed. "You really don't give me many reasons to assume otherwise."

"That's fair."

But here she was.

And they had bigger things to deal with. Even Luca knew that. His hurt feelings and anything else that might get in the way and complicate shit could wait a while. He was fine with that.

"And consider before you make another phone call," Penny said, pointing at the phone he had left sitting where he put it on speakerphone earlier, "that if Allegra or anyone else from her side of things manages to connect you to me right now, we are one step away from Naz, Roz, or—"

"I don't need the reminder. And I think we're safe."

Penny arched a brow. "Maybe, but *still* ... I take enough risks."

But not with them, he knew. Hell, she ran away to become an assassin just to protect them. Luca didn't think it was the right time to point that out, however.

But that gave him another thought.

"All these years, huh?"

Penny had been reaching for the handles of the duffle bag, but froze mid-grab. Her bright stare darted upward, slamming into his when she asked, "What are you talking about?"

"Naz's father knew for all these years. Where you were, I mean. What happened. Cross knew all of it because he orchestrated it."

A slow, steady stream of air left Penny's parted lips, but otherwise, she gave nothing away. Even when she replied, "It's not him I have to worry about here. He just signed a paper once—cleared up the details, so to speak. The rest was me."

"You don't think he has influence with one of the organizations currently hunting you down right now considering *he* was the one who brought you to The League?"

Penny's jaw flexed. "They're not the same as The Elite. Regardless of what they're doing right now, they're *not* the same even if their goal is a similar one."

"Your point?"

"They're the least of my worries. Like my ex-boss."

"Are you sure about that?"

Because he thought they might be the only real threat left when it came to her safety. She had already severely wounded The Elite as an organization—their hired dogs on Penny's trail were probably about as useless as the people in control of their leashes at the moment. The League was not the same. And the only connection between her and them that could be helpful was Cross Donati. He figured that was an important detail.

"Are we done talking?" Penny asked, snatching up the duffle bag. "Because if so, we need to go. No point in staying here longer than we need to. The city is buzzing right now."

Luca heard what she didn't say. "I know a place we could go for a couple of days, or whatever you need."

Far away from city lights.

"What I need," Penny muttered, "is time to let things work."

"What things?"

Her answer?

"Everything, Luca."

He wasn't surprised.

"We'll need a car," he called at her retreating back while he gathered his few possessions left in the room.

"And I bet you can get that figured out, too. Right?"

"Maybe."

Penny winked over her shoulder where she waited by the hotel room's door. "That's why I need you, Luca."

Right.

That was why.

· · ·

With a little time and inspiration, Luca could figure anything out or make shit work. Some might say he was resourceful, but he thought it was a lot simpler than that. Habit bred obsession, in his case, and he was a product of exactly that. He didn't like unanswered questions, of any kind, so he had taught himself how to find the answer to problems no matter the issue.

Penny needed a vehicle?

Last second?

No worries.

"Which unit is it again?" Penny asked.

"Three-oh-six. We're almost there."

The echoes of their footsteps carried down the long corridor of storage units. The wide—and tall at eight-feet—orange doors with silver numbers seemed to go on forever. He hadn't explained much about the vehicle they were there to get out of storage. Only that he knew where they could get one without much trouble. He was one of the few people who could head into the front office of the facility, give his first and last name and passcode, and be granted full access to every storage unit on the property connected to his surname.

"Is it yours?" she asked.

"Not really."

So to speak.

"Are you purposely being difficult?"

Luca grinned her way, saying again, "Not really."

Penny didn't even hesitate to swat at him, which Luca dodged easily. Just as fast, he came back into stride alongside her, slinging an arm over her shoulders to drag her close. Penny's laughter muffled against the arm of his jacket when he pressed a kiss to the top of her head. When he did finally let her go, although not too far because he kept their hands connected even if it was only by their pinkies, she didn't ask more.

Not about the car.

Or the storage place.

He was grateful; this shit wasn't simple, they didn't have the time to linger for a long explanation, and he really didn't care to get into all of it. The storage unit they were visiting wasn't his, but he—like every Puzza in the state—had access to it.

It was his father's. The Aston Martin Vanquish was one of his father's favorite—and least used—car in the man's fleet. Zeke liked to keep his many cars spread out across the state. From the Jeep he kept at the weekend townhouse, his parents sometimes used in the city to the expensive storage unit where the Vanquish stayed safe and mostly undriven.

Zeke only brought it out on special occasions. Luca didn't even have to call and ask his father whether or not the car was available. Not that he would—hell, the man wouldn't even know the vehicle was gone before he put it back.

When he put it back, that was.

The storage facility wouldn't bother to call Zeke, either. It wasn't unusual for people with wealth to have other people handle their business for them. Unless something seemed off or they had a reason to call, then they didn't.

It worked in Luca's favor.

He really didn't want to drag his father into this. The two still had other things to deal with, and he was sure Zeke's opinion would differ from his own about how to handle the entire Penny situation. He just didn't care to know that opinion. It made no difference to his own.

"Here we are," he said, releasing Penny from his grasp just long enough to punch in a code on the electronic lock for the unit housing his father's car.

"I just realized I didn't even ask what kind of car it is."

Luca gave her a wink, his smile growing wicked when he replied, "Oh, and that's the best part."

The large, metal door lifted to expose the Vanquish before Penny could even ask why. There was something to be said about the sexy, sleek lines of the shiny slate gray luxury car with its chrome accents and wheel rims that practically glittered under the automatic lights that turned on to greet them. It was like showing it off for the first time, every time.

The way Penny stared at the car as a low whistle cut past her lips said she liked it. A lot.

He could relate.

"Nice," she said.

Luca nodded. "I thought so."

"But that wasn't the best part."

He looked her way as he headed for the lockbox where he knew the spare set of keys was kept on the wall. "Why is that?"

"You still haven't told me where we're going."

Ah, yeah.

He liked having secrets, and she was fine with letting him work something out for a stay outside of the city—or even the state—as long as they were safe. His idea would serve all of that just fine.

"You'll find out soon," Luca said. "You never know, you might even get to pretend like the rest of this shit doesn't exist while you're there."

Penny only shook her head, but those eyes of hers told the truth. He didn't even know if she realized it, but with him, she was … happy. She smiled and it beamed. Who else made this woman laugh? He dared to believe he gave her some sense of joy. Even when they were running for their lives.

Couldn't forget *that*.

• • •

"Well, what do you think?" Luca asked.

Ahead of him, Penny spun a circle in front of the perfect view of the three-level lodge that his father had bought for Katya on their twentieth anniversary. Tucked away on ten acres of private, wooded land that the locals of the small Connecticut town had dubbed *Tori Mountain*, his parents had renovated the already existing cabin into a modern, spa-like experience to use for a weekend away.

Or longer.

There was even a pool.

Underground—in the basement, partially. A section of the basement was nothing more than a glass view of the mountain and the rough, winding dirt road leading out of it.

"It's perfect," Penny finally replied.

Her sigh echoed.

"Maybe we could pretend here, huh?"

Luca smiled. "Yeah, maybe."

He stayed leaning against the car, sneaky enough to shoot a text through on his phone while Penny's back was still turned. To Naz, his words simply read, *Connecticut lodge*. By the time she had turned around to face him again, Luca was already tucking away the phone before she knew what happened.

Penny would worry.

But other people were already doing that, and they had been worrying about her for a long damn time. Naz had asked to be kept updated. After all the shit Luca had already hidden from his friend—and still was in the case of the man's father—he figured he could at least do this.

What would it hurt?

He also did want Penny to just enjoy the lodge.

"And was that a stone chimney I saw?" Penny asked as he approached.

Luca laughed deeply. "Sure is—I can even light it up for you."

"Tell me there's a rug in front of the fireplace."

"Bearskin, babe. Canadian black bear."

Penny sighed again.

That time, it sounded like *sin*.

With tightness in his throat, all humor gone, Luca passed her by and said, "Let me get started on that, then."

She smirked. "You better."

• • •

If Luca's life depended on his ability to describe temptation, it would be the sight of Penny lounging on her side, head propped into the palm of her hand, in the middle of a large bearskin rug. The black fur surrounded her creamy curves from all angles. He immediately regretted the decision to indulge her request for wine when he dared to mention the wine cellar earlier.

Had he not went in search of the years she asked for, then his hands would still be plastered to the alabaster canvas of her skin. He'd nearly mapped all of her to his memory with nothing more than his fingertips. He knew there were more parts of her skin that were scarred and rough to the touch than perfect and silky. It would take him nothing at all to find the spots where she would shake and break the fastest.

Except he found new things to enjoy about Penny every time he had the luxury of fucking her. Something else for him to learn—because he just couldn't help himself.

"What's wrong?" Penny asked, falling to her back as Luca neared the side of the rug.

Chuckling to himself, he set the two wine glasses down to the floor beside the rug and then went about pouring the wine to an acceptable level in both. He'd at least had the foresight to uncork that shit downstairs and give the wine some time to breathe.

"Nothing," he murmured.

Penny hummed under her breath, pointing a single finger at him. "Liar. You even had a little knot right there between your eyebrows like you do when you get mad … or confused. They do a whole thing."

Luca glanced upward, freezing as he did so, muttering, "My eyebrows do a *thing?*"

A *whole* thing, apparently.

Penny pursed her lips into a pout, saying, "Well—"

"I wasn't mad."

"You definitely were. The eyebrows did the thing."

Fine.

Luca gave her a devilish smirk when he said, "I was annoyed—I could have been buried balls deep in you up here instead of digging around in the wine cellar for thirty minutes. My eyebrows must do the thing when I'm annoyed, too."

She had not been expecting that. Not if the way her cheeks heated, and the color rushed down the delicate column of her throat to the valley between her perfect tits, was any indication.

"I *love* that I can still make you do that," he told her.

Penny's gaze narrowed playfully below him. "At least you got my wine. Even if you did suffer blue balls *and* shrink—"

"*Hey.*"

Her pealing laughter had Luca darted down to capture Penny in his arms before she could even try to get away from him.

"*I was kidding!*" she shrieked.

It was already too late. He had Penny's wiggling body pinned in his arms. His fingertips raced down her side as her laughter came out higher from his tickles. He was pretty sure at least one of the wine glasses got knocked over in the process, but he didn't feel all that bad about it.

Her panting, uncontrollable giggles filled the space until he heard, "Oh, my God—*stop, please.*"

And he did.

Instantly.

Luca wasn't anywhere near being done with *touching* her, though. His hand dipped lower, his fingertip grazing her navel on the way by, before he found the hot, damp heaven between her thighs. Still wet—still sensitive to his touch—she opened for him the second he made his intention clear. The second his hand was flush against her sex, she pressed into him harder.

He had to tease her, though.

It was only fair.

He stroked the seam of her sex, circled her clit until she was nearly ready to blow, and even used only the tips of his fingers to fill her while he kept one arm locked around her. Then, she couldn't get more than what he gave.

"*Please,*" she gasped, her lips quivering against the underside of his jaw when she tried to turn in his arms. "I need to come ..."

"You will."

On his tongue. Around his dick. Whatever way he wanted to have her. She would come ... eventually.

Penny's next words were a whine. "You're such a—"

"Tease, yeah. Like you."

"I'll make sure to annoy you more often if it ends like this."

Her words were a breath. She'd already lost her air, and he was only *playing.*

Luca hadn't expected the weight of her words to be as heavy as they felt, though. Even if it wasn't her intention. Feeling her tremble around him when he finally stretched her full with three of his fingers, he swallowed hard and muttered, "Be here long enough to do it, then."

15.

PENNY could feel Luca's gaze on her the moment she broke the surface of the pool. Though it was only fifteen feet long, it did have a shallow and deeper end. Standing up and walking through the water to the marble stairs that led out of the pool, she couldn't help but smile at the sight of the man leaning against the sliding glass doors. Instead of coming closer as Penny climbed the stairs out of the pool, Luca stayed right where he was between the threshold of the pool room and the rest of the basement and wine cellar downstairs.

"Quite a view, huh?" she asked him.

She was talking about the glass wall of windows at the far end of the pool that overlooked the rear of the property and how the tops of the trees lower than their position seemed to go on for miles. Fog still clung to the tops of the trees, not yet ready to let go and drift off while the sun rose higher in the sky.

It was beautiful.

Every morning—three so far—that they spent at the lodge, Penny made sure to include a dip in the pool just so she could watch the fog roll off the trees.

"It certainly is," Luca returned, grinning deeply.

Except he didn't look at the windows. Hell, he didn't even look away from her. Penny had long since become comfortable in her own skin, and with sex. Or rather, the fact that in the right circumstances, she *could* enjoy sex.

Luca made it different.

He didn't just see parts of her—certainly not the parts she disliked the most about her body. Discoloration, scarring ... everything that made up *her*. He saw all of her. Each piece that made up an entire puzzle of a human being.

Of a woman.

And he made her feel like that, too. Like a woman who had more purpose than just sex even though he could spend hours devouring her. She was someone desired. He stared at her with hunger, and she felt it on every exposed inch of her body.

Especially walking out of that pool. Water fell down from her breasts and hair in droplets while the cold air pebbled her skin and nipples. Was someone really swimming if they weren't doing it naked?

Twisting more water from her hair, Penny came to stand in front of Luca with a smile. "Did you just come down here to stare at me?"

"Well—"

"Not that I don't like it. You give me an ego."

Luca laughed a sexy sound and leaned over to steal a quick kiss. Penny didn't even have time to react when she was still trying to wring water from her hair, and the kiss was over before it could begin. Another tease.

"You should have an ego," he replied, winking, "and no, that wasn't the only reason I came down here. Thank you very much."

Hmm.

Penny arched a brow. "Is there any news?"

He had contacts that he promised to put to use to find any information on what was happening in New York. Whether that information was about The League's movements, or whatever plans Allegra might have in the works, she would take it. Penny was running blind at the moment—hoping that her previous plans put the rest in motion while she was away. She didn't mind letting Luca do the legwork of finding info when his phone was apparently a burner, and untraceable.

Three days wasn't a lot of time to let shit happen, but that didn't mean it wouldn't, either. She figured it was better to know if something was going on sooner rather than later. If they could find out anything at all.

"Nothing big," Luca told her, shrugging as she pulled a large, white towel from the waiting rack beside the doors. Warm from the heated vent that constantly blew on the pile of towels to keep them ready to use, the soft cotton stopped Penny's shivers the second she had it wrapped around her frame. No longer naked, that didn't stop Luca from still admiring her. Only now, it was the tip of his finger tracing the exposed line of her shoulder. "A funeral is in progress, though. Or the planning of one."

"For my grandfather."

Luca nodded. "Yeah."

"I expected that."

"But there is something else," Luca said.

His tone dropped.

He also looked away.

"Something bad?" Penny asked first.

"No, but—"

"Something about New York?"

His gaze slammed back into hers. "We're going to have visitors. You should probably get dressed."

Penny's heart slammed hard in her chest. "Who?"

But she thought she probably already knew.

• • •

"You *lied* to me," Penny hissed, tossing the hoodie away that Luca tried to offer her. One of the over-sized black hoodies that she kept in her travel bag when she was working because it was a staple in her wardrobe. A *must*. Hoodies made everything better when she put one on and flipped up the hood—she could hide away—except right now. Nothing was good now. It might have been cold outside, but she didn't want to take something he tried to give her when she was pissed. Petty? *Maybe*. She was allowed her moments. "You made me think we were going to come here because it was safe, but really it was to get Naz and Roz—"

"Penny, stop it."

Luca's words weren't even sharp, but the way he glanced at her—those green-blue eyes of his piercing right through her rant with enough force to shove her next words back down her throat—had Penny quieting. Even if she did glare when she did it.

"I didn't lie," he said. "I only told Naz where we were in a way that he would understand. What he chose to do after that was out of my control. Shit, he didn't even tell me they were making the trip until he was already halfway here. You think Naz is stupid? He knew I would tell you. Don't worry—my friend knows where my loyalties are right now. He had to learn the hard way. Just like everybody else."

Penny stiffened as the sound of tires rolling against the gravel driveway leading up to the lodge reached her spot. She only needed to glance to the side to look out the windows on either side of the lodge's French front doors to see the approach of the black BMW. Tinted windows and distance kept her from seeing beyond the front windshield.

Her attention went back to Luca.

"What the hell did that shot about your loyalty mean?" she asked.

Luca was unphased at her attitude. "Wasn't a shot. Wasn't even a blow. It's the truth. I'm here because of you—I'm going to stay that way."

Well, then …

She still wanted to be mad. A part of her thought he *was* lying about Naz and Roz's arrival at the lodge. But nothing he said was a lie, and she knew it. It would be a low blow for her to push the line and call Luca on it when—above everyone—his intentions were always the best when it came to her. He didn't even try to pretend otherwise.

Not that she had the time to consider it. The approaching car was now parked twenty feet away from the front of the lodge, right beside the slate gray Vanquish.

"It's not safe for them to be here," she told him.

Penny headed for the front door to pull it open. Luca followed close behind, murmuring, "I know, and so do they. It's clearly a risk they're willing to take."

"Well, I'm *not*."

"Too late, Penny."

She didn't need to be told.

Silence settled over the property when they stepped out on the lodge's front porch. Across the gravel drive, Naz had already stepped out of the driver's seat and rounded the BMW to open the passenger door. Penny was stuck in place; frozen like a statue. She couldn't take her eyes off the woman who exited the car using her husband's hand to help.

Roz didn't look away from her, either.

Penny hadn't expected the moment when she came face to face with Rosalynn to be so … *quiet.* Or that her heart would feel as heavy as it did when Roz swallowed hard, and swiped away a stray tear that dared to fall down her cheek while her husband murmured something next to her. Roz nodded, glancing away from Penny for the first time to turn around and open the back door.

Naz leaned inside the vehicle, and Penny sucked in a shaky breath, asking, "They brought him, too?"

Little Cross, she meant.

Luca only shrugged. "Guess so."

God.

She wanted this.

She also knew it could be bad. Especially if someone followed them or—

"Just … say hello," Luca said softly, his hand finding the small of her back. It took nothing more than his touch for her to lean closer. "All you have to do is say hi."

Right. Of course, he would take her silence as a sign of nerves. He also wasn't wrong even if she was trying to deal with far more than her emotions.

But what about the rest?

Penny didn't have time to consider it. The second the Vans of a little boy hit the gravel, the rest disappeared. Little Cross walked just beyond the rear passenger door, laid eyes on Penny, and that was it for her. The kid beamed—his smile grew faster than her own, if she were being honest.

She was sure the rest of them hadn't been expecting the kid to look at her and immediately shout, "Penny!"

He darted away from his parents before they could even consider capturing him. His navy blue windbreaker matched the color of his khakis. He was a tornado of energy coming her way—without any care at all—and she couldn't help but laugh.

The two met at the bottom of the steps. She bent down with open arms that he rushed into for a hug, but then just as quickly pulled back to stare at her with those dark, familiar eyes.

"You're back," he said.

Penny smiled. "Not technically."

The little scrunch of his nose said the almost six-year-old didn't like that answer at all.

"Back?" she heard Naz ask.

Luca let out a sigh. "There are still some things to explain, man."

"That so?"

"Naz—"

"I get it, Luca."

He sounded like he did. It was also entirely possible to understand a situation and be pissed off about it, too. Penny and little Cross watched the exchange, but her attention drifted to the quiet woman watching from further away.

Roz didn't come as close as Naz had—she wasn't crying, but the water hadn't left her gaze, either. There was pain in her stare, but also joy. It dripped from the warm, *motherly* smile that curved Roz's lips the longer the two watched one another.

"Hey, Roz," Penny whispered.

She stood; little Cross let her go, but didn't move away. Roz, on the other hand, didn't move a muscle. Even when she replied, "Hey, Penny. A few years really ... grew you up, didn't it?"

Penny laughed, not expecting that. "Something like that."

In the same black cargo pants and crop top that she had been wearing the day before, Penny was sure she didn't look at all like the image of the young teenager that Roz had tried to save. She wasn't that girl anymore— this woman was someone else entirely. It was unfortunate that the woman who inspired Penny to find happiness so long ago hadn't been able to watch her transition into this person she became, but she hoped Roz would still love her the way she had when she needed it the most.

Because she still needed it. To love was human.

Penny had never been loved until these people—now she loved them entirely too much. She realized that only made her need their love, too.

Maybe that was why she told Roz, "Staying away was easy when I didn't have time to think about what I did when I left—I'm sorry I did it that way. I'm sorry I left without telling you why. You deserved better than that. I loved you more than that."

Roz blinked, and the tears fell. "It's okay."

"Is it?"

Because she didn't think so.

"I just want a hug, Penny," Roz said, smiling in that way of hers again. The way that made everything okay. "Can I have a hug?"

How could she say no?

16.

Luca

"MA said there's a pool," his godson said as Luca guided him beyond the front door of the lodge.

Naz walked ahead of his son, replying to the boy before Luca could say a thing, "And I told you that we weren't staying long enough to swim, my dude."

Cross sighed.

How did so much attitude fit into such a small human?

He kind of loved it.

At the same time, Luca was also too distracted with the scene they had left out in the driveway to really focus on the conversation happening between Cross and Naz. He reached for the door to close it, unaware that his friend was watching him as he took one last glance at Roz and Penny still locked in each other's embrace.

His sister had started crying, and Naz nodded toward the door. Luca got the hint, and pulled his nephew away from the two women to let them have their moment in private. And yet, even as he felt like he was intruding by watching them for another few seconds, he couldn't help himself.

Roz had waited a long time for this, but so had Penny. He didn't think people realized that—as confused and lonely and abandoned that they had felt for years, so had she. Just in her own ways.

"Look at you," he could see his sister say to Penny, her hands pressed against either side of the younger woman's face. "I thought you were dead."

He couldn't see Penny's reply, only the shake of her head. And that was enough for him, anyway. He didn't need to see more; he didn't feel the same urge to make sure everything was going to be okay if he closed the front door and let Penny out of his sight. That monster was a hard one to shake, but he was doing well about hiding it.

Mostly.

Naz told him differently when Luca finally closed the door only to turn around and come face to face with his best friend. Gone was his nephew— probably already raced ahead of his father when Naz decided to tell the boy where the pool was. Whether he swam or not was another story. Now, it was only him and Naz left in the front foyer of the lodge, and he knew just by the way his best friend stared at him that his distraction was not missed.

Stoned-faced, Naz's gaze drifted over Luca's shoulder to the closed door and then back to him without pause. Then, he asked, "You're close."

Luca blinked. "What?"

He didn't even know where to begin with that statement. Or how to take it, for that matter.

Naz didn't intend to make him wait to find out because he followed it up with, "You and Penny—the two of you are close. I saw it. How you stare; when you touch … I saw it, Luca."

Shit.

Yeah.

Something else he hadn't gotten to.

"Is there *anything* else you want to tell me?" Naz asked, his fiery stare never wavering from Luca even though his tone kept calm.

Luca was fucking tired.

Of a lot of damn things.

Serving everyone else's hand but his own was high on that list—even if that meant betraying people who meant the world and more to him. Like his own godfather.

"It's more than just Penny," Luca told his friend, "but I can start there."

"Start," Naz deadpanned.

"Well—"

"No, I mean … *start*, Luca." Naz shrugged, adding, "And try to make it quick—we really aren't staying long. I just promised my wife I wouldn't lie anymore and when you texted Connecticut, I knew where you were, and I couldn't *not* tell Roz. And guess how that worked out."

Luca didn't bother to hide his grin. "Seems obvious."

"*Start.*"

"Relax—I just …" Luca let out a hard breath and shoved his fists into the pockets of his jeans so that he had them under control. His nerves always showed in his hands first. Naz had told him that more than once. "I could love that girl—I think I already do."

Naz blinked, muttering a soft, "*Huh.*"

That was it.

Just *huh.*

"That's what you say to—"

Naz tipped his head to the side, his stare lowering from Luca's like he was thinking about something when he replied, "There's really nothing else that I need to—or should—say when you lay it out to me like that. If that's what it is, that's what it is."

"You don't feel any kind of way about her or before when she was living with you guys—"

"I know you. I know who you are. I don't need to ask that. I already know the answer to that, Luca."

He breathed easier … because despite being who he was, he never wanted to be a monster, either. It was a lot harder to be the man he was—who came from the people and place he did—while also maintaining compassion. All of their moral compasses were a bit broken. That didn't mean they always had to act like it.

"You said to start," Naz pointed out. "So what else did you have to tell me?"

For a second, Luca hesitated.

He even started to ask, "Shouldn't we go find Cross? The pool is—"

"It's protected by a passcode. He's probably staring at it through the glass doors, scowling and looking like my father, but a mini version that constantly mocks me."

Jesus Christ.

"He also acts a hell of a lot like you."

Naz's lips dared to twitch with a smirk. "Yeah, well—"

"It was your father," Luca decided to say with no warning. He said it when his friend was amused and slightly distracted because he hoped it would lessen the blow. He wanted to give Naz a chance to absorb the news without the hard impact. "It was your father that helped Penny get away all those years ago—he signed her contract with The League which included paying the *millions* for her training. Cross did all of that."

And more.

But that wasn't the important bit.

"He's known where she was this entire time," Luca added quieter.

Naz said nothing. His stare turned so cold, it burned. The way he stood a little straighter, jaw tensing like he might speak before he decided to say nothing telling Luca everything he needed to know. Naz was pissed.

"All this time?" his friend finally asked.

Luca nodded once, ignoring the way his mouth wanted to close around the words he spoke. "Since day one, man. I'm sorry."

"When did you know?"

"The day I got back from Nevada."

Naz blew out a hard breath and swung away from Luca, his hand coming up to cup his lower face as he growled something into his palm. Then, he turned back around, waving that same hand wildly when he snapped, "That's why he did what he did … all the things he did. Telling me to focus somewhere else but Penny—so my workaround was *you*. But then he made me so busy that you were basically out there on your own while I handled business. And just when shit starts to come to a head, when she's getting closer, and I might stick my nose where it didn't belong, he decided to put me into his seat to head the family. Because what boss has time to be everywhere when he can barely even be at home, right?"

Luca swallowed the uncomfortable knot in his throat. "I don't think his intentions were bad—that's not your father, you know?"

"That doesn't change what he did!"

Naz's shout had Luca quieting instantly. Because what else could he do? Sometimes, anger just was what it was. They had to treat it like it, too.

"Why didn't you tell—"

"He asked me not to," Luca replied, already knowing good and well what his friend was going to ask. "I didn't make promises, but I also had to prioritize the shit I needed to handle. Penny needed to come first, and I was running out of time to—"

"Find her," Naz finished for him, nodding. "Yeah, I know."

"She's being hunted from all sides and has a million-dollar bounty on her head. I keep trying to figure out the way this is going to end ..." Luca trailed off, laughing dryly before he added, "But every end I imagine is never a good one, Naz."

"You don't know that. She's a ghost—to the world, she doesn't exist. Just because she's real doesn't mean she's already dead. They haven't even come close to catching her yet."

"And that doesn't mean anything," Luca said.

Naz shrugged. "It also hasn't meant a bad thing."

Well ...

• • •

"He didn't believe me."

Luca didn't move from his spot at the rear of the foyer where he leaned against the wall. "What do you mean?"

Penny shook her head, the wavy strands of her white-blonde hair moving with the action. "Cross. I told him I would see him soon. He didn't say that he thought I was lying, but—"

"He rarely has to."

The kid just had a ... *look*.

The goodbyes hadn't been easy, and Naz also hadn't lied. His sister and her family didn't stay long—less than an hour from arrival to departure, actually. Naz managed to pull the short reunion together for his wife, but he couldn't do more than was safe. Being *anywhere* Penny was until this finally ended was more than dangerous.

It was stupid.

But there Luca was—just fine.

"But I get it," Penny said, turning around to face Luca as she shrugged almost helplessly. "I wouldn't believe me, either."

Luca raised a single brow, asking, "You seem less angry now."

"At you?"

"Well—"

"They shouldn't have come here."

"I have little say in what Naz and my sister do."

After locking the lodge's front door—not that it would do much to keep them safe if someone really wanted to get through it—Penny came to stand in front of Luca at the other side of the foyer. Her silence said a lot. He figured, so did his.

Eventually, she said, "I know, Luca."

"For what it's worth," he murmured, leaning closer until their lips grazed with every word he spoke, "I believed you. When you told him you would see him soon—I believed you."

"Maybe you're just a fool."

She kissed him once.

Soft and teasing.

Luca dragged in a shuddering breath when Penny pulled away, replying, "I heard that happens sometimes."

Penny dared to smile—a sight that warmed his heart like nobody would ever know—when she asked him, "What happens?"

"That love makes fools of us all."

She stilled, gaze darting to his. He swallowed the ache rising from his chest into his throat, refusing to move until she said *something*. Anything at all.

"Is that what this is?" she eventually asked. "When I can't breathe, when there's nothing but you, and when I see you in my dreams—is that what this is, *love?*"

He couldn't answer that for her, only say, "That's what it is for me."

She took a second—pulled in a hitched breath when her hand came up to lay flat against where his T-shirt stretched across his chest.

Then, she was kissing him again. Only this time, there was nothing to tease.

• • •

The taste of chlorine hit the back of Luca's throat when he came to lean against the sliding glass door leading into the pool. At the far end of the room, still in the calm, crystal blue water, Penny used her folded arms as a perch for her shin on the side of the pool. Her icy hair hung in wet waves down her naked back as her shoulders rose and fell with steady breaths. It was the only way Luca could tell she was even awake considering she didn't move or speak otherwise, and he couldn't see her face.

She faced the windows overlooking the rear of the property where the basement of the lodge was exposed. He wasn't close enough to appreciate the view like she could at the moment, but he also didn't need to in order to know what she was seeing. The inky sky dotted with bright, twinkling stars. A mountain of treetops hat lifted and lowered for miles. Lush, green land that went on forever—an endless possibility, really.

The view truly was the best part of the lodge even if Luca's view wasn't the same as Penny's. He still thought his current view was damn good, too.

God.

This woman was doing crazy things to him. Even watching her while he did nothing but be silent was something to appreciate. And yet, he was the first to break the silence because he just … had to know.

"Are you still angry?" Luca questioned.

She was due to have her feelings about the reunion with her adoptive family. He would never suggest anything different. And he knew most of her anger was born from a place of fear—her concern for the people she cared about the most seemed to overweigh almost everything else for Penny. Even her own feelings and wants.

"I wasn't … *angry*," she finally replied, although he barely heard her over the humming of the pool's filtration system. That's how quiet she was—he didn't like it a bit. "I'm just tired."

Hell.

Luca understood that.

All too well.

"I parked the car around the side of the lodge. Inside the trail with all the bags in the trunk," he added, still feeling the weight of the keys inside the pocket of his jeans. "So, that's done."

The only other exit from the lodge's property, actually. The dirt road was more like a path, a long way to the bottom of the private property, and not nearly as comfortable of a drive. But she wanted to leave in the morning, and Luca mentioned the other road in case she might want to use that to go.

Surprise, she did.

"Good," she heard Penny say absently.

"Hey."

She didn't move.

Not even a peep.

"Penny, *hey*—"

"Could we come back here—someday when … things are better?"

Luca stiffened at her question. Not because he didn't like the idea, but more because her request was the first time that he could remember her wanting to make … *plans*. Future plans. She suggested an *after* would come—a time when all of this was over, but even doubts lingered in the back of his mind when her mission sometimes seemed impossible.

At least, not without a tragic ending.

Luca didn't answer her back right away, instead he rounded the front of the pool to walk along the side to the other end where she waited for him. Penny even turned around in the water to watch him as he came closer, using her arms to prop her up against the side edge until he was right behind her. Luca stared down at the beautiful, broken, *perfect* woman that had changed so much about his life.

More than she would ever know. He didn't know where to begin to try and explain, after all.

Without a word, he kneeled and pressed a kiss to her wet lips that still tasted of the pool and that vanilla lip balm she'd been using lately. The soft stroke of her mouth against his answered him back, and he told her, "We'll do whatever you want, whenever you want."

And that was that.

Because the truth was easy. What else needed to be said?

Penny grinned against his next kiss, mumbling to him, "Get in the fucking pool, Luca."

Absolutely.

He wouldn't say no to that.

Luca made a pile of clothes alongside Penny's near the window before he dove into the deeper end of the pool where his lover had started to wade water. By the time he broke the surface of the water back at the edge of the pool, Penny was already moving toward him.

His back hit the wall when her hot mouth found his. His arms kept them steady along the side of the pool while her long legs tangled around his waist under the water. There was nothing quite like the sting of this woman's nails pulling across his skin while her pussy rubbed a rhythm against his cock and made him hard. Her tongue teased his, flicking inside his mouth just long enough to let him get a taste before pulling out of reach.

She lifted higher on his body. Luca moved with her, tilting his head back, so she could drop another one of those hot kisses against his mouth while her hand worked between their bodies. First, she stroked his cock, but then she had him pressing between her thighs. The blunt head of his dick slipped into the silky heat of her sex—and he was floating high in nothing but sensation and bliss.

Breath gone.

Nerves snapping.

Chest aching.

The pool bit into his back when he only kept one hand at the edge to keep them steady. His other hand found the fleshy roundness of her ass. His fingers dug in as she rode him, and he used that grip to yank her harder into his cock, so he could get those breathless whines escaping her lips just the way he liked.

She watched him through heavy lids and long lashes. She'd lean in just close enough for him to nibble against her jaw, or even closer when she wanted him biting that spot on the side of her neck where she didn't even care if he left teeth marks behind. The faster they fucked, the more the water made waves against the edge of the pool, some reaching high enough to splash onto the tiles.

The closer Penny came to her orgasm, the more she wanted to touch him. Her hand rested to his cheek before her fingertips dragged over the line of his jaw. When those fingers of hers came close to his mouth, he sucked them in for a taste. His teeth scraped along the digits as Penny let out a hard breath when she came down on his dick a little harder.

"*Come*," he told her. "Get what you want, baby. You know I got it."

He always did.

Luca could have stayed like that forever.

Fucking Penny.

Taking in her life.

Wrapped up with her.

Together in whatever their love was.

He'd stay like that.

Always.

Reality was a bitch, though.

She came with a heavy hand. A screech of tire against gravel, and smoke bombs that were thrown through the windows of the lodge. It all happened so fast that at first, neither of the two in the pool even knew what was happening.

"Fuck," Luca hissed.

Penny was already reaching for the side of the pool to pull herself from the water when the first smoke bomb was thrown into the downstairs. Her wide, wild blue gaze darted to his when she screamed, "*Move!*"

The stomp of feet accompanied the smoke and confusion. Luca just did what he was told and pulled his body from the water, naked and cold. He barely felt it at all, but he heard every step and shout coming closer as the smoke started to crawl over the pool at the far end. The only thing that worked to their favor was the smoke bombs clouded the intruders' view of their escape.

Penny grabbed the clothes. Luca busted out the windows with a chair. The rush of air from the outside pulled the smoke toward the windows even faster. He couldn't see anything—especially not the pale beauty who had just been at his side.

He felt her hand, though,

Finding his.

She pulled him through to the outside. It was then that he finally understood why she wanted him to move the car and for them to have a second exit plan.

Nowhere was safe.

Not even paradise.

17.

LUCA drove the Vanquish through the small, winding dirt road that led out from the rear of the lodge's property. Penny didn't even care to argue about who was behind the wheel because the man had proved himself in that regard on more than one occasion.

The vehicle jumped, and the tires slid on the path more than once, but even so, Luca kept the car under control. Going at a speed that would have frightened a weaker woman sitting in the passenger seat, Penny, however, wasn't bothered.

"Are you going to say something?" Luca asked.

She glanced away from the bag in her lap—the only one Luca put in the backseat and not in the trunk; *hers*, with her weapons and other items she liked to have close—to see his knuckles were ghostly white from the tight grip he had on the steering wheel. But other than his stronghold on the vehicle, the man was unfazed.

He stared at her, waiting.

Penny didn't know what kind of response he wanted, saying, "It was just a matter of time before someone found us there. That they would find *you*—if you're not around to be found, then you must be with me. That should tell you something right there."

It took Luca a moment.

Penny waited him out.

"The League attacked us tonight," he murmured, gaze darting back to the road after their brief exchange.

He couldn't see it since his attention was back on whatever was coming at them on the dirt road, but Penny still shrugged. "The Elite don't know about your connection to me maybe beyond my past, and I've not connected myself to that in any way."

Except him.

But her mother's people didn't know that. Only the organization she had been working for that was now out there hunting her like a fucking dog. As if *she* was the one doing something wrong when she was just trying to finish what they had allowed her to start. Just because they allowed it didn't mean they also got a say on when it ended.

Full stop.

She respected The League for what they had done with her—for what they gave *to* her. And she would not go out of her way to purposely hurt anyone from an organization that for years had been the only family she had to her name. That wouldn't stop her from doing whatever she needed to do to meet her end goal.

They could get in line.

Or get out of the way.

"*Shit*," Luca snarled.

His harsh exclamation accompanied the screech of the Vanquish's wheels when Luca slammed on the brakes without warning. Penny jerked forward violently with only inches to spare before her face smashed into the dash. She didn't have her seatbelt on because honestly, that had been one of the last things on her mind. The only thing that saved her from getting a broken face—or worse—was Luca's arm that caught her right under her throat.

Not that it was an easy impact. His fucking arm was like a bar, and when she hit against him with her chest, all of her breath went with it.

"*Sorry*," she heard him mutter. "Fuck, are you ok—"

She didn't hear the rest of his concern because in the midst of being thrown forward, she had finally gotten a glimpse of what waited for them around a bend on the dirt road. She realized then why Luca had slammed on the brakes as hard as he did, and why her fucking distraction with their conversation and the bag in her lap had been foolish.

Of course, The League had a backup. Why wouldn't they? Penny knew how they worked. She was one of them.

The lights of the Vanquish illuminated the man standing directly in the middle of the road. Though the road wasn't that big, to begin with, the bend had been widened, it seemed. For what reason, Penny wasn't sure but it allowed the other vehicle—with lights turned off—to park off to the side. Out of the way.

"I almost killed him," Luca said under his breath, staring out the window at Cree who still stood in the middle of the road staring at the two of them in the car like he didn't have a problem in the world. Hell, the man even *smiled*.

That was most unsettling of all.

"Apparently," Penny mumbled when Cree pointed a single finger at her and then crooked it as if to say *come here*, "I'm not the only one around here that trusts your judgment when it comes to driving."

Luca's head snapped her way. "What?"

It wasn't important.

Just a thought.

Penny reached for the handle on the door at the same time Luca asked, "You're not seriously going out there to talk to him, are you?"

With only Luca's T-shirt that she had managed to throw on once they were in the car, and her panties, Penny didn't even bother to reply to him before she stepped out into the cool night air. She figured, what did it matter—why waste time stating the obvious when her actions would speak for her?

She understood Luca's worry.

Penny didn't share it.

If the man waiting for her on the dirt road wanted Penny dead, then she would already be buried six feet under where no one would ever find her body again. That was the thing ... she knew the truth about what was happening in her life right now. Other people needed to catch up, too.

Rocks bit into the soles of Penny's bare feet as she approached Cree with no weapon in her hand and no threat on her lips. She even smiled—like him.

"Did you come to collect the bounty?" she asked him. "Or is this ... League business."

Cree folded his hands at his back as she came to a stop only three feet away. He didn't comment on her lack of clothes. He didn't even give her appearance a second look; his gaze stayed on her face. "I hope you know that putting a bounty out was probably the stupidest thing I have ever seen someone of your position do to themselves."

"But how hard has it been to find me with a hundred other people looking, too? Didn't they get in your way at all?"

Cree's jaw flexed. It was subtle, but she saw it. Penny wouldn't let it pass, adding quietly, "Bounties make people greedy—especially a million-dollar one on the head of a legend. See, you did that. You made me into *that*, Cree. Don't fault me for doing the rest because I could. You don't need to tell me what I already know. No one is going out of their way to help The League right now with that kind of money on the line."

A resigned huff left the man as he turned his head to the side, staring at the parked vehicle on the side of the road. With windows tinted black on all four corners, she couldn't tell if there was someone else inside the two-door, black coupe or not.

Did it matter?

They weren't getting out.

Cree's brown gaze swung back to Penny when he told her, "Dare was right—you were a pet project I let get out of control, but he was wrong, too ... when you break already broken people, Penny, it only teaches them that they can and will survive. This was inevitable."

Her brow dipped. "What?"

"You don't have much time—they're maybe forty seconds behind if they followed instructions. And the team did. They always do."

Right.

She was starting to understand. After all, it was only Penny who had constantly pushed and broke the rules when they didn't suit her. The rest got to be sheep.

Cree tipped his chin toward the Vanquish, muttering, "I had to make this look good. At least, I could do that for you."

He was going to let them go. She knew that the second she stepped out of the car, and he hadn't shot her dead on the spot, but still ... a part of her dared to wonder if that would be the case. Nothing in this life was ever promised.

"Do they know what you're doing right now?" she asked, referring to the people probably racing down the dirt path to catch up.

But also the people he left in Nevada.

Dare, too.

Wherever he was.

Cree surveyed the dark sky, shrugging his broad shoulders under the black, cotton long-sleeve he wore. "They should, but—"

"I'm doing what's right."

His stare slammed back into hers when he replied, "Well, I just don't think you're wrong. And I'm making choices here ... ones I might not be able to take back. Go, Penny. Before you can't."

Luca slammed on the horn—had he rolled down the window to listen? It didn't make much of a difference, and Penny didn't bother to say goodbye to Cree—or even a thank you—before she ran back to the car. She didn't even get the door closed before Luca had taken the vehicle out of park and slammed on the gas. Cree had just managed to step out of the way when the car sped past, rocks and dirt spitting out from the tires on the way by.

The only thing on Penny's mind?

She wanted this to end.

It needed to be over.

"Luca?"

If he looked her way, she couldn't tell. Penny was too busy staring out the window and letting her mind wander.

"What, babe?"

He was going to argue.

She was willing to fight.

For this, always.

"You need to go home," Penny said, finally looking his way. Luca's mouth immediately opened to refuse, but she was quick to say, "I can't finish this with you, and I'm not the girl that needs to be saved, anyway. It'll be better if you're—"

His hand slammed into the steering wheel palm first.

Penny didn't even flinch.

"Why—I can *help*."

He could.

But that also meant ... "I don't want you to; I want to come back to you, Luca. Don't you understand? I'm not running away. I'm running back."

His attention drifted between the steering wheel and her. She already knew how this would end between them. He would agree; she wouldn't have to say much to make it happen. He loved her.

This man *loved* her. Luca would do anything for her.

He already had.

• • •

Penny stared at the gate that led into a large, three-level suburban home tucked away in a gated community that seemed safe and quiet. Then again, with only the street lamps on to give the place any life, she knew the place looked a lot different in the daylight.

It wasn't her first time here, after all.

She should have been thinking about the man in the house that she had come here to see, but instead, her mind kept drifting back to Luca. He let her keep the car, but she dropped him off two miles away from his parents' home. She would have figured out something if he didn't let her keep the Vanquish, but he hadn't seemed concerned.

He simply said, "Dad's already gonna kill me for the lodge—who gives a fuck about the car?"

And then he kissed her.

She could still feel the way his lips molded against hers when he leaned inside the opened driver's window to say goodbye. Even the strokes of his tongue and the graze of his lips were still imprinted on her memory long after he was gone.

She still felt it.

Still tasted him.

She hung onto that memory even when the gate guarding the driveway's entrance started to open. Luca's kiss still teased her senses and felt like a ghost on her lips as the car crawled closer and closer to the Donati family home.

Luca didn't know—she hadn't told him—but asking him to go home and let her finish her job alone wasn't easy. In fact, it was the hardest thing she had needed to do yet when he was ... still her safe place at the end of the day. But she wanted him to keep being that for her.

This needed to happen.

Penny hadn't expected to find Cross waiting for her on the front porch of his large home. She certainly hadn't thought Nazio would be standing there beside his father when she parked the Vanquish, either.

Neither man seemed shocked when she stepped out of the vehicle. Penny was sure she was still quite a sight—despite getting fully dressed—with her wild hair, calm demeanor, and sure stride. She could have lost her life tonight; it was just another night for her, though.

They didn't know that.

"I told you—"

"Zeke will not be pleased the Vanquish was used," Cross muttered, interrupting whatever his son was about to tell him.

Naz's lips pressed in a thin line as he glanced sideways at his father. "That's not even close to being the most important thing happening right now, and you know it."

"I've said what I've said, Naz."

"Dad—"

"I did what I did."

Ah.

Penny came to a stop at the bottom of the stairs leading up to the porch at the same time she realized Naz being here wasn't entirely coincidence. It seemed the man had finally found out the truth about his father's involvement with her disappearance years ago, and he had come to talk about it.

Bad timing.

She was here for her dues, too.

"The lodge was attacked—The League came up on us," Penny told Naz. "Three hours after you guys left."

"Is Luca—"

"Probably dealing with his father now."

Naz flinched.

Next to him, Cross simply stared at Penny. "Why are you here? That's a better question."

Wasn't it?

"This needs to end," she told her former boss, "but I think I need your help."

He'd helped her once.

She was willing to ask again.

18.

Luca

THE familiar ceiling above his head should have been a comfort to Luca when he woke up, but it wasn't. He spent too many seconds following the curvy swirls in the plaster with his gaze and breathing in the scent of his parents' home. A mix of cinnamon and fresh apples. Scents his mother loved, he knew.

He'd barely been awake more than a minute before a throat cleared to his left. He didn't need to turn his head to know his father was watching him from the living room entryway. He still did nonetheless.

Zeke stared back, quiet.

The mug of coffee in his father's palms, the rim rolling with steam, dared to make Luca's mouth water at the thought of something hot and bitter. Zeke didn't offer the mug, or even a word, where he leaned in pajama pants and a plain tee while Luca righted himself to a sitting position on the couch.

"What time is it?" he asked.

Zeke sucked air through his teeth, replying, "Little after ten."

Luca blinked. "In the morning?"

"It's not dark outside, is it?"

He didn't bother to check the window. He was more surprised at the fact his father was still in pajamas considering the time. It told Luca a lot without his father needing to say a word.

"How much was lost?" Zeke asked.

Yeah.

Shit.

Just like that, the night before came rushing back. Not that he really forgot but in his haste to sleep off the exhaustion that carried his footsteps up to his parents' home, he hadn't stopped to explain very much when Luca and Katya came out of their bedroom to find him using his key to get in.

Clearly, Zeke found a way to fill in the blanks.

"What do you know about what's going on?" he asked his father.

Zeke lifted one shoulder. "As much as Cross."

Well, then …

"The Vanquish is gone," Luca muttered. "Or it will be."

"And?"

"I don't know about the lodge in—"

"I had that entire place designed for your mother, Luca."

111

He winced. Zeke wasn't even *angry*—the dip in his tone and almost resigned delivery spoke of disappointment. How long had he been doing that to his father—disappointing the man? Shit, even when he didn't try.

"I'll replace everything," Luca said, pushing up to stand from the couch. He tossed the afghan blanket to the tan-colored, leather arm, and faced his father again. "Or Naz will. Penny, maybe. We have time to figure out the details."

"Do we?"

He didn't know what his father wanted him to say. No doubt, there was a whole spiel that Zeke was holding back. He wasn't sure what he could do about that, either.

His father didn't hold back for long.

"What in the hell are you doing?" his father demanded. "You disappear for weeks and days at a time—I can count on one hand the times you've called your mother in the past couple of months. How did you go from hunting down an invisible girl to—"

"I never hunted her. I only wanted to find her, Dad."

Zeke's tension didn't ease. "To what cost? Have you really asked that yet? *Really* considered it?"

"Yes and no."

Because it didn't matter.

"Luca …" Zeke dragged in a hard breath, stopping only when Luca felt like all the air had been sucked from the room. He didn't pretend to be perfect—he could be selfish even if some people might call him selfless. It was why Zeke knew better than to ask for an apology when Luca wouldn't say he was sorry. "This isn't what I wanted for you, son. This—what you're doing. I wanted you to be—"

"It's what I wanted, and I can't be like you. I won't be like you."

"What does that mean?"

Now or never, he supposed.

Right wasn't always easy.

Penny taught him that.

"You were like me once—doing what you wanted, being who you wanted. The only difference between me and you is that you let your father decide your future, but we both know you won't do that to me, too."

Zeke said nothing.

Luca understood why.

The values of Cosa Nostra had been at the base of their family's entire life. Everything about the way they invited people to their home to the color car his father could drive was determined by the rules of made men.

Of *mafia*.

His father would do and say a lot of things—but he would never speak against *la famiglia*. Not even to tell his son that he was right.

112

That was fine.

Silence could still be respect.

"Maybe I just want to be more than this," Luca told his father. "Or maybe I just don't want to be told what I *have* to be."

"Does being more also mean being alive, too?" Zeke returned, softer than Luca expected.

He didn't get the chance to answer. His mother slipped into the entryway beside Zeke, the cordless phone to their home pressed against her palm where she covered the receiver end.

"It's Naz," she said, her gaze flicking to Zeke and then back to her son. "He said he was told to call here to find you."

Luca didn't hesitate to step across the room and take the phone from his mother. "Thanks, Ma."

"You busy?"

It was the first thing Naz asked when Luca said hello. Was he busy? He thought about Penny, and how he only ever wanted to help. It was sadly ironic that in the end, helping meant doing *nothing*. That killed him.

Still, Luca replied to his friend, "No, man, I'm not busy."

● ● ●

"I was at my father's place when she got there," Naz said.

Although his words were clear, his gaze was distant, stuck on the little boy who sat beyond the doorway of his mother's music room. Little Cross either didn't know his father and uncle were watching him, or the kid just didn't care. He tinkered with the keys as a familiar tune echoed from the brown bear perched on the edge of the piano. Soon enough, his tinkering of the keys turned into a matching melody that he played by ear.

Huh.

Luca missed that—somehow, his godson went from showing interest and taking lessons to seeking a piano out and making music. It was that moment when he realized just how much of his time and life had been wrapped up in a game he wasn't sure he would be able to win. Or even … a game he still wanted to play, for that matter.

He didn't want to keep missing things.

"Luca," Naz murmured.

He dragged a hand through his hair and tried to shrug off the distraction when his attention came back to his friend. "Sorry—she was there, you said?"

"I was already there—I had business to settle with my father. Personal and otherwise."

Luca let out a soft *damn*. Then, he asked, "How was that, anyway?"

"*Hard.*"

Yeah, he bet. Luca wasn't the only one dealing with issues relating to the most important man in his life. *Still.* Was that maybe the fate of men like them? Fathers and sons that pushed and pulled just a little too much from one another.

"She asked him to help again," Naz said low, like he didn't want the little boy in the music room or even the woman down the hall to hear. "Penny asked my father to help her."

"How?"

"I don't know."

Luca's gaze caught and held his best friend's. "How the fuck do you *not* know when you were there?"

"He asked me to leave."

And he did, Luca knew.

Left.

"And that's it?" Luca asked. "Now I what ... I *wait?*"

Naz lifted one shoulder, his stare drifting back to his son. "We wait, and we keep people safe, we handle business ... we help. Because if we're doing what we need to do, then they don't have to worry about us while they do whatever it is they need to do."

Right.

To Luca, that only meant he was still in the dark.

Still playing the game.

19.

"I was going to tell you to relax, but then I realized you look just fine sitting there and didn't need me to tell you anything at all."

Penny's stare drifted away from the burry trees to the man sitting beside her in the back of a black town car that had arrived earlier at his mansion to pick them both up. "Men tend to do that a lot, don't they?"

"Do what?" Cross asked.

"Think women constantly need your help—even in little ways."

"It could also be a way we've learned to show we care."

"Because it makes men feel better in some way to *provide*. Even if whatever their providing isn't really needed."

Cross dared to crack a smile, clearly amused by Penny's challenging stance to what was a kind gesture. She would never say it was anything but, either. That didn't mean she couldn't also see the intentions of others—but especially men—for exactly what they were at the end of the day. Not that she thought this man had any bad intentions for her, but she also couldn't change the part of her that would forever be protective of her very self.

Besides, she didn't think it was wrong to believe women should be taught to love, serve, and care for themselves before a man ever did. After all, how could a woman be expected to know what she wanted from a man when she didn't even know what she wanted for herself?

"If I wanted to be a real prick just because I could," Cross told her, his amusement lifting one brow high while he regarded her, "then I would make a comment about women wanting to fetch good husbands who can and do provide, but that's not my style. And my wife would pickle my balls."

Even Penny smiled, then.

Cross's grin stretched wider, as though he had gotten what he wanted from her. Maybe he did—some sign of life that she was there despite what they were driving toward. "Relax, Penny. This needed to happen. At least … consider that you're going to finally know how this will end. One way or the other. There's solace in that—try to find it."

She let out a breath she hadn't realized she was holding. *Damn.* Maybe she had needed him to tell her what she didn't want to hear.

"How much longer?" she asked.

A man in the front seat, a trusted enforcer for the Donati crime family, spoke up before his boss could answer the question.

"Ten more minutes to the meeting spot," he said.

Cross gave her another look. Penny only turned back to the window where she could watch the trees. It was easier. She thought about things a lot less … *felt* less about everything. It was the only way she could do this.

• • •

It had been Cross's idea to make contact with The League—to extend the offer of a sit down so that two organizations could come together for a peaceful discussion on the current situation. She hadn't been agreeable … to say the least.

At first.

But the man explained the benefits to what he had called a *meeting on no man's land*. No weapons. No guards but for their drivers. Out in the open … mostly. Because apparently a man's word was everything in their world, and if both sides gave their promise to a non-violent meeting simply to discuss a possible alternative option to hunting Penny down like a dog, then she would be foolish not to take the opportunity.

Again, so Cross said.

As she had been the one to seek him out and ask for his help, who was she to say that he wasn't right? She was trying to trust him.

As much as she could.

Penny was surprised to see Dare followed through on his promise to only bring as many people as the Donati side of things. They made two, and their driver made a third. Cree stood a few feet behind Dare with his hands folded at his back, as usual. The man who didn't exit the black four-door SUV kept his window rolled down with a sharp gaze on the new arrivals.

Penny and Cross stepped out of their vehicle at the end of a dirt road that stopped at the mouth of a large farming field far outside of New York City's limits. Rows of gold wheat swayed like waves against the black backdrop of the open sky. She might have admired the many stars that dotted the sky and how peaceful it all seemed far away from the noise and movement of the city, but she couldn't.

Not considering the circumstances.

"I appreciate you agreeing to this meeting, Dare," Cross said.

The League's highest-ranking member didn't reply. Not at first. His piercing stare followed Penny's every footstep until she and her companion were only five feet away from the man standing in his pressed slacks and red, silk button-down. Not an inch of Dare suggested the man was anything but calm and unbothered, but she knew that couldn't be true.

After everything … he must hate her.

She didn't blame him.

"I had my reasons for agreeing," Dare murmured, finally giving Cross his attention. "And let me say, it had very little to do with *you*."

Cross nodded. "That's fair."

Penny asked what Cross didn't—what she felt was the most obvious and important thing. "Then, why did you agree to this?"

Dare's stare darted back to her and for a second, silence answered her back. She couldn't even hear her own breath or heartbeat as the man considered her. If he *really* wanted her dead, she had no doubt that she would already be six feet under.

So, what was he waiting for?

"Because I have something to say—the only offer I am willing to make," Dare said, "and there was no other way for *me* to tell you."

"I did make it hard for you to catch up, didn't I?"

Dare chuckled. "And yet here we are ..."

Exactly.

"The offer?" Penny asked.

"It's more like the consequences, Penny," her former handler explained. "We're going to allow you to finish what you started with The Elite ... *without* interference from our organization."

Her next exhale stuttered, but she didn't have time to reply.

Dare was quick to add, "However, The League will be available and ready to collect on the bounty of a former member once your task is completed. You have two weeks without any contact or issues from us to kill Allegra Dunsworth, but that's it. We will come to collect one way or another when the two weeks are up. Someone will be there, Penny. Look for them."

Beside her in the darkness, Cross stiffened. Yet, the man didn't speak. This wasn't about him, after all. He had simply made this meeting possible for her to do with what she wanted.

He'd been right.

She was here to learn how it would end.

The only illumination of the quiet people, dirt road and wheat field came from the moon overhead and the dimmed lights of their vehicle still running twenty paces back. Penny did find solace in the silence and the finality of it all, even as she wished Cree would speak where he stood behind Dare, or that she felt better about the weight now sitting inside her heart.

Instead, she was numb when she told Dare, "I'll take that deal."

• • •

"Penny—"

"Do you have a phone?" she interrupted, not giving Cross a chance to say a thing after they had watched the taillights of the SUV disappear down the dirt road.

She didn't have a reason to believe Dare would return with Cree and their driver to go back on his word and finish the job of killing her early, but ...

"Of course, I have a phone," Cross replied.

"I wasn't sure. I thought maybe you hadn't brought one—no way to track you."

He rolled his eyes. "You work with too many hackers."

"Your son is a hacker."

Sort of.

Point was, if he wanted to state the obvious, then so could she.

Cross scowled, then, muttering, "I know the risk. What do you need a phone for?"

That was a tricky answer, and not particularly one she wanted to give. Yet, as Cross stared at her from the side, waiting for a viable reason that she would want to use his phone at a time like this, she decided to be honest.

"I'd really like to speak to Luca," she admitted.

It was selfish. She wouldn't be able to tell Luca anything about what was happening. Not without sending him into a panic that might put him in danger. She wouldn't do that. He was going to ask, though.

She knew it.

And yet ...

"Could I use your phone?" she asked quietly.

Cross let out a sigh as he dug for the phone that he eventually produced to her. Penny took the device he dangled without comment, but he was quick to ask, "He's a good man, isn't he?"

She blinked, not expecting that.

He didn't give her time to react before he added, "And he wants to be yours—your man, or so I was told. How is he supposed to do that now?"

Truth was power.

But truth was also pain.

Penny hid hers well even as he took the phone without reply to his statements. Instead, she asked, "Where should I call? I don't think he has a phone and—"

"I heard he's been staying with my son. I assume you know Nazio's home phone number. He's never changed it."

She did know it.

Penny dialed the number without much thought to what she would say when someone answered the phone. Someone did—it was Roz. Through a painful whisper, she asked for the man who had given her everything to live for more times than he probably knew.

She didn't know what she would say to him, either. And because of that, when Luca's dark *Penny* echoed through the phone's speaker, she lied.

But she also told the truth.

"I love you, Luca—I'll see you soon."

20.

Penny

THE sniffles, soft murmurs, and footsteps followed the sea of the grieving that walked behind a casket made of gold. From the bars the ten pallbearers used to lift the ornate, gaudy casket to the lids that had shut Charles Hatheway into his coffin.

Well ...

Someone who didn't know the infected, poisonous history of her family ... they might assume she would feel something watching a church full of people follow her grandfather's casket out to the waiting hearse that would deliver him to the crypt deep within a New Jersey cemetery where the rest of his family rotted together.

As rotten as him.

After all, he learned his vile ways from somewhere—or someone. To her, the abuse seemed like a disease that had chased her family for generations. Spreading and killing and ruining everything that it touched.

Even her.

No, she felt nothing as she watched the casket leave the church. She didn't even care to look back over her shoulder at the altar where the family and friends of Charles had left a memorial in his body's wake. The mountains of flowers and framed photographs that had followed her grandfather's life from boyhood to a senior widower. From an innocent child to ... a monster.

One of many.

Instead, Penny stayed in the pew, pretending to fuss with the purse in her lap as the last few stragglers headed down the aisle after the family. She couldn't help but hear their conversation as the women passed. Not that they could see her interest—the black, birdcage veil attached to the large-rimmed hat kept her face covered well enough when she had added a handkerchief to the mix just for good measure.

And for show, obviously.

"Gilles wasn't here, I noticed," the taller of the two women said to her friend.

The other one snickered. "Oh, I think Allegra can count her marriage over before it even began, Lydia."

Before the women said anything else, they were already gone. Drifting down the aisle, their voices turning to whispers as they neared other people who might hear their unsavory conversation. Not a soul had dared to say one word about the fact that the senator had not shown up for his fiancée's father's funeral.

Statements were being made.

Apparently.

Penny no longer cared about the business or life of Allegra's fake fiancé. Everything about the senator suggested the man had simply gotten tangled up in a web of lies—nothing more, and nothing less. He certainly wasn't attached to The Elite or their business beyond his connection to her mother, and that had quickly fallen apart. She was sure the man had gone through a whole education about who exactly Allegra Dunsworth really was over the past few weeks.

She hoped his daughters were safe, now.

But that was all.

All that remained in the church besides the dying flowers on the altar and the scent of incense lingering in the air was Penny and the nuns starting to clean up at the front. There had been a large crowd at the funeral, but she expected that. She wondered if that was purposeful on the part of Allegra—another way to keep herself safe in the mess that she had created—or was it just the influence of a horrible man.

Hell, even tyrants were adored.

Why wouldn't a monster be loved, too?

At the far end of the church, she heard a man tell one of the women, "Well, we better hurry if we're going to see them carry him into the crypt."

Yes.

Penny had to hurry now, too. She had a long-overdue meeting with a woman, and Allegra always did hate to wait.

• • •

"I'll miss you, Daddy."

How sweet …

Those were the first words that Penny had heard her mother speak over the course of the day—from a safe distance, of course—that she believed were true. Probably because Allegra was finally alone for the first time since arriving at the funeral in the back of a blacked-out town car with black sunglasses and a matching hat to keep anyone from seeing just how many layers of makeup she had caked on her face.

Was it getting hard to sleep?

Did dreams keep her awake?

Were they nightmares?

Penny wanted to ask as she rounded the final corner from the left-wing of the crypt that would meet the right—it was there that Charles' golden casket had been left alongside his wife's, parents', and siblings' graves.

121

Instead, she said nothing as she moved like a ghost around the corner to find Allegra moving just a step away from the casket where it sat on a marble pedestal.

She made no sound.

There was no warning.

Like all of her kills before Allegra—each one that led up to her—the white ghost swept in with the same grace, danger, and beauty that had accompanied every murder she had ever made. She had never planned to treat her mother with any less respect—and lack of empathy—that she had for any other pedophile that met their end by her hand.

Because the woman wasn't different.

Pain was *pain,* and God above knew that Allegra hadn't been anything to Penny for a long time ... not a mother; nothing but a living, breathing scar she felt forced to wear. Another reminder of a shameful, dirty secret that had left her believing she was broken and unwanted for more than half her life.

Not worthy.

Not good enough.

Used.

There should have been more satisfaction inside Penny's thundering heart when Allegra turned back slightly—just enough to catch sight of her daughter raising the nine-millimeter with the long end of the silencer pointed directly at her face.

Instead, what she felt was fear.

It clawed through her chest and lungs like a hungry, angry bear woken from its cave before the spring. All of her muscles locked, tensing into hard balls; boils ready to spring, and even her breath caught in her throat with a painful slice right down her windpipe.

The fear was still real.

Still *violent.*

It was also fleeting; a blip in the raging war of what was Penny's mind whenever she stared into the eyes of the woman who had both birthed her and took away her will to live. All because she could—because Penny was *hers.*

Allegra's piercing, cold stare widened when Penny told her mother, "I thought you might like to die with the only person you ever loved—so die with him."

Allegra didn't speak.

Couldn't.

Not when Penny didn't give her the chance. Those painted-red lips of her mother's opened with words that she would never get to say. And what was more beautiful was the fact that Penny didn't wonder what those words might have been when the bullet from her gun plugged into Allegra's forehead.

Two seconds later, her mother's body hit the floor. It was the only noise left in the crypt, the dull thud carrying down the massive corridors, around the corner to where she knew people were waiting fifty feet away for Allegra to come back out.

But there were two wings.

Two ways in.

Not that Penny had time to absorb the impact of her finally ending what had been started far too many years ago. She had to leave—the white ghost left in much the same way that she came—but she did take the chance to glance back as the skirt of her black dress whipped wildly around her legs when she turned back for the left-wing.

Allegra's dead stare and the blood pooling down between her eyes, ruining the canvas of heavy makeup, stared back.

"Goodbye, Allegra," she whispered.

She'd done it.

Faced her demon.

Slayed the monster.

It should be over.

Penny should have been happy.

Angry.

Anything.

Right then, she was … nothing.

Empty.

Alone.

• • •

Penny was grateful for the cobblestone walkway that led up the final hill at the far end of the cemetery. It led to the same entrance she had used that connected to the side of the church. A quick way to the crypt, but not one that the hearse could drive while the hundreds of people followed behind.

Heels and grass were never friends, but at least the cobblestone made things slightly easier for Penny at the end of her trek out of the cemetery. With a little more conscious effort, that was, because nothing about cobblestone and heels were friends, either.

She blamed her distraction with moving fast—but also staying upright—for why she didn't see the figure waiting on the other side of the hill when she came up over it. Hollers for help had already started to echo for Allegra when Penny first exited the left wing. A siren wailed in the distance—was it for the dead woman who couldn't be saved?

"Was it like I promised it would be?" he asked.

Penny came to a standstill on the pathway, her skirt billowing from the wind as her head snapped up. She didn't even react to snatch the hat that blew off her head in the wind that had picked up a lot more since she first arrived at the church that morning.

Cree waited for an answer. A gun rested in his right hand.

Penny rocked against the wind, her slight sway the only thing that moved between her and Cree for more seconds than she cared to count. The scent of ammonia from the boxed, black hair dye that she had ruined her white-blonde locks with the night before danced over her face when strands of her hair whipped against her skin.

She swallowed.

Her words.

The air.

Those few final seconds ...

"Do you remember," he asked her, "when I made that promise?"

She did.

Two months into her training at The League, swallowed by her fear, with bloodshot eyes, and tears that tasted like salt staining her lips, he promised she would feel nothing when she killed Allegra. Cree had bent over her in the darkness of a room that she never wanted to even smell again and told her she could have the thing she wanted the most—to feel *nothing* when it was finally the end.

"I was scared," Penny told him.

Cree dared to smile, as tiny and fast as it was. "And then?"

"She was gone."

"And you felt—"

"Nothing," Penny said, her words a rushed ache leaving her lips. "Nothing at all."

His expression softened even as he raised his weapon. His dark eyes met hers, and she found remorse there—waiting for her, though he wouldn't offer it in words. That was okay.

"When you killed her, or two weeks—whichever came first," he reminded her.

"Tell Dare I'm not sorry."

Cree nodded once. "You shouldn't be."

Ever.

She was owed this.

"Dare made me a deal, too," Cree said, his finger wrapping the trigger. "You only have to die, Penny ... and maybe then you can live."

He pulled the trigger back. The last thing Penny remembered was coughing and the taste of blood thick in her clogged airpipe as she stared up at a bright blue sky, and rolling white clouds. She heard a click—a digital *ding* as her heart fought to keep beating.

She felt every single one.

And how they slowed.

Penny would have liked to say that she had no regrets at the moment of her death, but that was a lie.

She regretted not saying goodbye.

21.

Luca

THERE was nothing quite like the streets of New York City, mid-week, at the end of a long workday. Often congested, and yet fast-paced in a blink, driving in that mess could make a normal man insane. He kind of liked it.

Luca could thank his father for demanding he learn how to drive in downtown Manhattan during early Monday morning traffic when he hadn't even known how to back a vehicle up at that point. And it was one of the only times that he couldn't focus long enough to *think*.

At least, not too deep. That was better, lately.

Thinking led him down too many rabbit holes—Luca didn't enjoy the helpless feeling he was left with every time he was reminded that Penny was … somewhere.

Somewhere without him.

Luca let those thoughts drift away as he finally rounded onto the block where he had to meet up with a Donati capo. Being the go-between to pick up payments so the capos weren't forced into the same spot when things in the city were tense was just one way Luca was helping to keep shit steady for Naz and *la famiglia*.

He didn't mind.

It kept him busy, too.

And if this was the only way he could help to keep the streets of New York from becoming anymore bloodier than they already were, then this was what he was happy to do. Simple as that.

Before long, Luca was able to pull his car to the side of the street where temporary parking allowed him to sit for five minutes or less. He sent off a quick text—a confirmation that he was outside the coffee shop where the capo spent his evenings in a rear office handling paperwork.

Luca didn't expect the capo to bring out the money—the dues owed to the new, sitting Doanti boss. He was right. A familiar family enforcer stepped out of the alley at the side of the coffee shop, telling Luca he had probably exited the business from a rear door. He didn't linger at the open window of Luca's latest buy—a new, two-door Mercedes that was blacked-out from the rims to the front windshield.

Money could make shit move in little time. He figured it was about time that he started spending some dollars. What good was it sitting there doing nothing, anyway?

It was also another way for him to distract himself from the giant hole in his life. A black space that seemed to be sucking all the good energy he had left with every passing second that he tried to pretend it wasn't there.

He assumed this was what it felt like to be heartbroken—a little empty, lost, and too quiet. Not quite right.

"Thanks," he told the enforcer when the man passed an envelope into the car. Luca packed it away in a bag on the passenger seat, and was already maneuvering the car out of the parking spot by the time the man had turned to leave. He gave the enforcer a two-fingered wave but didn't glance the man's way to see if it was returned.

Just as he pulled the car back onto the road, the Bluetooth in the car connected a call from the newest cell phone he had picked up to keep in contact with the important people who needed him. Or those he was paying to keep him up-to-date on information.

The number on the screen told him he was dealing with the latter.

"Keys," Luca greeted when he picked up the call. "Tell me the good news, man."

He drummed his fingers against the steering wheel as the car came to a stop behind a white SUV at a red light. *Good news* was reaching—he mostly expected the same news Keys had been giving him for days when it came to Penny and any possible sightings or word about the white ghost.

"Where are you?" the hacker asked.

"What's wrong?"

It wasn't unusual for Keys to ask Luca about his position when the man called—he was convinced it was because the hacker just couldn't help himself and everything was a challenge. Even finding Luca's digital footprint down to the goddamn millisecond.

It was strange for the man to be so soft-spoken … so *unsure*.

"Luca—"

He swallowed hard, his fingers wrapping the leather of the steering wheel until his knuckles turned white from the pressure. *When was that light going to turn green? "Keys."*

"The bounty's been collected, man. The bounty for the white ghost. It was just announced on a vanishing forum with digital proof—for a cost, of course."

"What the fuck does that mean?"

"Luca—"

"*What does that mean?*"

"It's a sealed file of a single photograph—it's her; if she wasn't dead, she would have been pretty soon after. Confirmed by a second witness on a another vanishing forum. The bounty is claimed—it's been paid. She's dead."

He had a lot of questions. Details he would never have. A horn blared behind him because the light was finally green, it seemed.

His vision was blurry as wet lines made tracks down his cheeks to his clenched jaw. He really only wanted to know one thing more than anything else.

Why.

That wouldn't be answered, either.

• • •

There was a stillness in the darkness that Luca appreciated. The quiet looming of shadows when the sun finally started to fall beyond a treeline was one of his favorite sights to see. He tried to show respect to the end of every day by taking a moment to watch it go because it meant he would soon be given the gift of seeing another start anew.

Except he didn't find the usual solace at the end of a day as he stared over the rear property of his family's home. He wasn't sure why Zeke and Katya's home was where everyone—from Naz and Roz to even Cross and his wife, Catherine—gathered, but they did. Food was cooked as calls were made and hushed tones turned to angry yells. Between friends, fathers and sons … shit, Luca even wanted to rage at himself.

They looked for her.

All of them tried—every man who had a contact they could pull *tried* to find her. Hospitals, morgues, organizations, and even walk-in clinics were called and given the same questions. None had seen the blonde, blue-eyed woman they asked about—Penny was a ghost all over again.

"Still nothing," Naz said when he stepped out onto the rear veranda of Luca's parents' home. In the wicker rocking chair, Cross finally glanced away from the cigar he had been working on lighting while Luca was lost in his thoughts and the oncoming night. "A new day is coming—let it be a restart."

Luca didn't even look the man's way when he muttered, "A restart to *what?*"

Because for him, life looked a little too dark now. How was he supposed to restart anything when he had barely even been able to begin in the first place?

He'd not been really living until he found Penny again … and now he didn't have her at all.

"Dad," Naz murmured, making Luca realize he still wasn't alone despite how he kept falling back into his thoughts. "Leave it alone. I think you've done enough."

Cross sighed, shaking his head and repeating, "Let it be a restart."

22.

"THEY certainly make doing our job … *difficult.*"

"Quite aware," came the murmur of another voice. "But as they have reminded this hospital time and time again, *they* also have a job to do."

"They could make a better effort not to impede ours. And how many times are you going to tell them she's non-responsive? Cop after cop can come into this room and ask her questions, but clearly she isn't answering them, Carter."

"They think she's … someone."

"Someone?"

"Someone," the male voice responded quieter like maybe he was worried someone else might overhear.

Penny *wanted* to blink, especially when the bright white circle moved beyond the vision of her one eye and then the other, but she couldn't. In fact, she quickly realized she couldn't do *anything*. And while her hearing seemed to be taking in the strange, unknown voices around her, the fuzzy darkness allowed her no sight other than whatever that *light* was.

Hey, she wanted to say, *help me*.

"You're seeing this, right?" the woman asked.

"I am."

"Do you think—"

"Reflexes, maybe. It's been a month. While her reconstructed valves in her heart have taken well, and the ventilator has allowed her body to rest after the trauma of the heart surgeries… this coma wasn't induced, Trin. Studies have shown time and time again that some activity is just … *activity*. Nerves that are awake, or brain waves running on autopilot. Like an electronic—"

"Dr. Morrisey, I know how this works."

Well, then.

But at least Penny had figured out part of the mystery.

Heart surgery.

Surgery.

On her heart.

And not one—but surgeries.

She was in a hospital. One with a name she didn't know being treated by doctors and nurses that didn't know her … if their earlier discussion meant what she thought it did. The news also explained the constant *beep-beep-beep* in the background coming from various corners of a room she couldn't properly see.

"Her lips are quite dry—would you grab a cup and one of the stick sponges for me?"

"*You're* going to moisten her—"

"Why wouldn't I?" the man asked. "She's a patient—I'm already here."

While Penny was interested in trying to decipher the dynamic between the doctor and the nurse, she was also starting to see shapes. *And color.* Not clearly—the edges were still quite fuzzy, she wasn't able to blink, but things were ... better.

The shadowy figure that moved away from the bed was a giant, pale green blob while the white one leaning in closer to Penny murmured, "I've tapped your lids open for the moment. If you are capable of hearing me at the moment because your pupils are reacting beyond the usual dilation, then you should know you've been in the hospital for a month. And you will be here for months more yet. The tube in your throat supplying the air to your lungs will be removed this week—should you wake up sooner, try to remember its there. It makes our job far easier when we aren't trying to fight with a patient attempting to rip it out."

Huh.

The doctor continued on, saying, "That bullet you took to your heart did some serious damage, and it is only because we have the best heart surgeon in the country that you are alive. Because you certainly were not when you first arrived, Miss Doe."

Miss Doe—

Oh.

Right.

Penny wasn't surprised that her identity was unknown—which probably explained talk of the officers who were making the job of her doctors and nurses more difficult than it needed to be.

The white blob of the doctor had started to clear in Penny's vision, but not enough that she was capable of discerning the features of his face beyond a smile that curved his fuzzy mouth. For some reason, that smile felt *kind.*

Something she should trust.

"What were you doing there anyway, hmm?" he asked. "Why were you on the other side of a cemetery where a murder had just happened only a hundred yards away?"

A hum followed the question.

And then, softer, he asked, "Or was it all coincidence?"

She didn't think he expected an answer. Not that she could give him one. A click, and the squeak of shoes had the doctor moving away from Penny.

She realized then that she was starting to *feel* something, too. The graze of soft, careful fingers on her face as a sticky sound pulled away from her skin.

Then, the room was dark again.

And the nurse was back. "Your water and stick sponge."

"Thanks."

"Have you told them, yet?"

"Told them what?" the doctor asked.

"The cops," the woman replied. "They asked to be notified if there was any change in her appearance. Not that I expect *men* to notice when it's only a month's worth of growth, but her roots ... they're a different color. It's not black, but it might not be what it was supposed to be, either. A black, chemical dye can sometimes affect the color of the first few inches of new growth. Especially if the hair was quite light, to begin with."

Silence answered the nurse.

But then, the doctor replied, "They'll notice eventually. I doubt her natural hair color is in any way related to the fact she was shot in the heart at a close range."

The beeps became louder soon after, and Penny drifted away from the voices. Toward the rhythmic pump of her heartbeats. A steady sound, but different, she knew.

It sounded different.

But hell ... at least it was beating.

• • •

"I've been told you've made remarkable progress in the last month, Miss Doe. Brain function is returning, and you're even showing some communication at times. So, today we're going to try answering a few questions, and then maybe I can finally put together the pieces of this puzzle you seem to be. Blink once for yes, and twice for no. Do you understand?"

Penny, propped up in the hospital bed so that she had a clear vision of the end of the bed and the detective standing there with his notepad in hand, did nothing. She didn't blink, grunt, or otherwise. If they brought the right doctor or nurse in, then she might consider it.

But not while a cop was there.

Two months in a constate state of helplessness being fed through a tube was not what Penny had wanted, but she also hadn't been given a choice. And since her identity was still a mystery to the hospital workers and the police, they had begun working more and more towards a recovery where she was capable of decent communication.

She understood.

She didn't always comply.

"Do you understand?" the man asked again.

He'd introduced himself when he first came into the room, but she didn't care to remember his name when there was a revolving door of officers who came to speak to her, or *about* her, for that matter. He was just one of many, and not that important. The man was only doing his job, and in a way, help her, but that wasn't how this would work.

It couldn't.

Penny was a ghost.

She would always be, now.

God.

She wasn't even supposed to *be*—she shouldn't exist. The agreement to forfeit her life for the ability to kill her mother without interference had been final. Yet, there she was … very much alive.

Penny couldn't waste the chance. Not when it might mean keeping a promise she never should have made in the first place. Not when it might mean turning a lie she had told someone else into a truth that she–

"Excuse me a moment," the cop said, stopping Penny's thoughts from going any further. She almost wanted to laugh at his politeness in the fact of her—well, her complete lack of response—but she couldn't. The only thing she could do now was blink, breathe, *think,* and lay in a damn bed.

And she wasn't answering questions.

Not a single one.

• • •

Footsteps pulled Penny from a restless sleep. Still propped up in the bed, she watched the doctor—the one everyone simply called *Carter*—approach the side of Penny's bed. The papers in his hands shuffled a bit before he placed them out of her line of sight. He'd had the nurses remove her feeding tube earlier, explaining it away with the promise of soft food soon to test her swallowing. It hadn't been a pleasant experience, she had more nerve sensitivity than she'd realized, when they pulled the tube out.

She hoped he wasn't there to tell her they would be putting it back in.

Other than an occasional check, the nurses and doctors didn't visit her at night. Especially not after she had been moved from Intensive Care. The police came around less often, but now it was dedicated officers tasked to her case.

Despite weeks upon weeks of drugs that kept her mind hazy and clouded with chemicals, after she had started to come out of the coma, her sleep came and went in strange bursts that never seemed to be enough.

No matter how hard she tried.

It helped once the nurses started opening the shades in the room to allow the natural light of the day to come and go. At least then, Penny actually had a concept of time and night and day.

"Evening," the man murmured, leaning over her bed to fidget with things she couldn't see. Not that it mattered—he told her what he was doing. "I'm removing your oxygen and pulse sensors, and then I'm going to turn off the machines. You're not going to need them shortly, for one thing. But also, because we don't want anyone running in here and making a scene as you come to."

Her mind tried to catch up, but being unable to speak and only a blink or two for yes and no … well, she didn't have much to work with.

"I suppose you're wondering why I'm doing this, but that's not really important. Fact is, he found you … and things worked to my favor."

He?

How was this *he?*

God, she wished she could talk.

"I'm shutting off the IV now," Carter explained, "and in a few minutes, you're already going to notice a difference. There was more to your concoction of medications than the nurses realized, but they eventually stopped questioning why I was the one who wanted to ready all your vials."

A beep sounded before the background noise of the machine stopped altogether.

Then, Carter leaned down and smiled in Penny's line of vision as he explained, "The paralytic in your IV is going to wear off, and you will be walking in twenty minutes. Not well, mind you, but walking all the same. It'll be completely out of your system within the hour. However, you don't have that much time to leave before someone realizes the living Jane Doe in room two-oh-four is miraculously walking, talking, and capable of being questioned by police."

Penny's gaze flicked lower to where the doctor played with an item that he flipped between two fingers.

A penny.

The coin danced around his fingers as her stare went back to his face. The doctor sat the penny down in the same general direction that he had put the papers.

"Take everything when you go—you might need it someday," he told her. "You'll need extensive and intensive care outside of this hospital, but I can't help you beyond what I already have. I was told you wouldn't need much help beyond this, anyway. Apparently, you're capable of finding your way back to the people who love and need you. Good luck."

Penny watched the doctor walk away at the same time she was finally able to start feeling the muscles in her throat. She swallowed back the words she wouldn't be able to say even if she tried, and instead fixed her attention on the clock. She watched every single minute pass. Until the tips of her fingers prickled with what reminded her of bee stings, and she was finally able to flex her toes again.

Twenty minutes wasn't enough. She stumbled out of the bed. Busted her mouth on the way down, too. She wiped at the blood with a shaky, weak hand as she used her other to grasp on the side of the bed and pull her weight up. Her attempt to be as quiet as possible was pointless when every action was followed by a grunt or a groan.

Eventually, she found what the good doctor had left on the bedside table with the penny. Papers. A contract, actually.

The League, it read at the top. She recognized the seal of the organization, and underneath, her name had been written in her own handwriting on a line just for her.

Except across the white paper was a red stamp—*VOID*.

She took the contract and the penny. The flaring, agonizing pain in the middle of her chest had Penny clutching at her own body to ease the sharp stabs that came with every step. Still, somehow, she made it out of the room.

And even the hallway.

She followed the signs, found a stairwell, and eventually an exit. Darkness met her on the outside, and cold, fresh air that she pulled into her burning lungs.

She was alive.

Free.

And going home.

23.

Luca

WHEN it was so early in the morning that there was still dew on the grass, Luca didn't feel so guilty about wishing he wasn't so fast to say yes about babysitting his nephew while Roz headed to her first prenatal appointment. Pretty soon, he was going to have another niece or nephew and he hadn't been expecting the news.

Neither was his sister or her husband, apparently.

Life had a funny way of working, though. He'd learned that especially in the past months as his life seemed to ground to a halt yet it was impossible to ignore the way everyone else kept going on around him. The thing about Luca …

Well, he was drawn to life.

Always had been.

It was why he lived fast, chased impossible things, and felt most alive next to a woman who the rest of the world said didn't exist. All of those things gave him a sense of life—of *realness*. He couldn't hide away and wallow in a pit of his own misery and hell when life kept drawing him back out into the daylight and fresh air.

Life like his family.

"Thanks again," Roz said on the back deck where she stood with Luca. "I know it was late notice and—"

"It's fine," he was quick to interject, though he didn't take his eyes off little Cross. His godson kicked the soccer ball from their side of the property to the middle never breaking stride or stumbling over his feet. It was a new thing he seemed to like—Luca had volunteered to coach a team, if needed. "No place I'd rather be."

The lie came out easy.

There were arms he would rather be wrapped in. A smile he would love to see teasing him again. Blue eyes—cerulean clear—that he could still see when he closed his own haunted his every peaceful moment.

"They haven't found her, have they?" Roz asked. "Still nothing?"

She had stopped asking after a couple of weeks. He was surprised she even asked now, really. When none of their contacts could find Penny after the declaration of a claimed bounty … he had started to think that was the point. They didn't want even her body found.

"Nothing," he murmured.

And not for a lack of trying.

Except leads ran cold and politics and policies kept them from doing things above board which only made shit harder when they didn't even know where to begin. A part of him wanted to bring her home—even a piece of her—for his own selfish reasons.

He would never tell his sister that, though. He would never say he kept looking even when he truly believed there was nothing to look for because *he* needed to have a part of her with him. He didn't keep looking because Roz wanted closure. He did it for himself.

"But it's not over," he added.

More for her benefit than his.

Roz nodded, turning back for the house. Luca pivoted with her if only to make sure she didn't trip on the damn lip of the back door's threshold. It wouldn't be the first time that happened, but he didn't want to risk her doing it while she was pregnant, too.

"Okay, well, I better get Naz out of the shower, or we're going to be late for—"

"*Penny!*"

Luca swung back around at his nephew's sudden shout. It took him a second to find the form that stumbled out of the treeline at the rear of the property. In his distraction with the conversation, he had missed the fact that Cross had kicked the ball to the other side of the back lawn almost to the trees.

Of course, the boy saw her first.

Luca didn't wonder if it *was* Penny—even the messy, ratty black hair would have made someone else pause as far away as he stood. But he didn't. Every part of him had thought she was dead up until that moment. He'd denied it outwardly to anyone else that asked until he just stopped saying anything at all.

And yet, right then …

Every part of him knew she was alive.

It was *her.*

"Oh, my *God,*" his sister breathed.

Luca didn't even take the stairs. The running start helped to launch him over the railing of the deck. He hit the ground already running. Roz's footsteps beat against the wood of the deck's stairs when he was already halfway across the backyard.

Unfortunately, he also got to watch as Penny's knees hit the grass, and the red splotch in the front of the loose gown she wore spread wider. Little Cross was already in front of her, his words carrying back in the breeze to Luca's spot.

"You came back," he told her.

Penny's laughter was weak, but *real.* "Of course, I did."

"Because you never wanted to leave."

"*Ever.*"

"Why are you bleeding?" Cross asked next, his voice pitching higher.

Luca was almost to them, so he was quick to shout, "Go get your father, buddy! Go tell him we need help!"

His nephew didn't question him. Luca was able to catch Penny as she was falling to the side. Instead of meeting the ground, her shoulder and back tucked along his legs as he wrapped his arms around her. He had a lot of questions, but none of them wanted to come out when tired blue eyes blinked upward and met his.

Instead, he kissed her.

Leaning down, while his sister found the ground beside them and a little boy shouted for his father, he found something beautiful against the lips of his greatest treasure. His impossible wish. He felt her mouth curve against his, and the chapped texture of her lips moved with his. It was only when her damp, dirty hands found the sides of his face that Luca pulled back a bit.

There was too much blood.

He was trying to figure out *why*.

Then, her trembling fingers ghosted over his smiling lips—because despite the worry and sadness in his heart at seeing her in such a state—he couldn't help the happiness swelling in his heart, either. For the first time, Luca truly understood what it meant to be *overjoyed*.

And it was overwhelming.

"What are you doing?" he asked her.

And where the fuck was Naz with help?

Like his sister could read his mind, Roz whispered to Luca, "Cross just got inside—Naz will only be a few more minutes."

"We need a clean towel—*something*," Luca muttered. "Me and Naz can get her in the house but—"

"I'll run in and find something."

"Okay, thanks."

"I'll be right back, Penny," Roz told the woman shivering in Luca's arms.

"I'm fine," Penny said in a breath that rattled on the exhale, "just tired."

But that wasn't good, either. And the bloody gash on her chest was now more visible as she laid in his arms on the damp grass. He was grateful for the privacy of his best friend's yard and regretted every single thought he'd had earlier about wishing he could be anywhere else.

"I *am* fine," she promised. "I haven't slept in fifty-two hours and—"

"Your chest is bleeding."

"I shouldn't have taken the trails. A root caught me when I slipped. That's all."

God.

He could laugh.

137

Her flippant, yet breathless, assurances were *crazy*. Yet, she made them like she expected no fight from him.

"What are you doing?" he asked her.

She was still touching his lips, the black strands of her faded box-dyed hair sticking to the pale skin of her face and throat. Not once had she looked away from him.

"Anything," she replied softly. "I want to do everything I couldn't before."

He would let her. Hell, he'd be right there doing whatever she wanted with her.

"I kept my promise," Penny said. "To everyone, Luca. Even you."

She had. He couldn't deny that. And God above knew that he loved her more because of it, too.

But did he ever expect anything different? Luca couldn't pretend that Penny was the average woman—certainly the exception. Beyond, even. Exceptional. She walked through hell, and then went back for more with a smile. And here she was, saying she wanted to be all of those things with him.

With a wound in her chest.

While she bled in his arms.

"I just want you," he eventually replied. "All I ever wanted was *you*."

He wouldn't let her go.

Not now.

Not ever.

Penny smiled wider, then, her lips trembling when she told him, "And now we can start over."

It took Luca a second.

Those words echoed; they were a reminder of something he had been told two months ago when he first learned the bounty was claimed. His godfather's promise that had left him so unsettled for more reasons than he was able to explain.

Like a restart, Cross had said.

"Can't we start over?" Penny asked him. "I want an … *after*."

"And I'll give you one."

Nothing else mattered.

It never would.

ABOUT THE AUTHOR

Bethany-Kris is a Canadian author, lover of much, and mother to four sons, three cats, and four dogs. A small town in Eastern Canada where she was born and raised is where she has always called home. With her boys under her feet, a snuggling cat, barking dogs, and a spouse calling over his shoulder, she is nearly always writing something ... when she can find the time.

Find Bethany-Kris at her:

www.bethanykris.com

OTHER BOOKS

The After Another Trilogy

One Step After Another
One Breath After Another
One Second After Another

Boykov Bratva

Fractured Ties
Essence of Fear

The Guzzi Legacy

Corrado
Alessio
Chris
Beni
Bene
Marcus

Renzo + Lucia

Privilege
Harbor
Contempt
Forever
Cusp
Renzo + Lucia: The Complete Trilogy

Andino + Haven

Duty
Vow
One Last Time
Andino + Haven: The Complete Duet

John + Siena

Loyalty
Disgrace
John + Siena: The Complete Duet
John + Siena: Extended

Cross + Catherine

Always
Revere
Unruly
The Companion
Naz & Roz

Guzzi Duet

Unraveled, Book One
Entangled, Book Two
Cara & Gian: The Complete Duet

DeLuca Duet

Waste of Worth: Part One
Worth of Waste: Part Two

Filthy Marcellos

Antony
Lucian
Giovanni
Dante
Legacy
A Very Marcello Christmas
The Complete Collection

Donati Bloodlines

Thin Lies
Thin Lines
Thin Lives
Behind the Bloodlines
The Complete Trilogy

Standalone Titles

Pink
Pretty Lies
Dirty Pool
Effortless
Inflict
Cozen
Captivated
Dishonored

Seasons of Betrayal

Where the Sun Hides
Where the Snow Falls
Where the Wind Whispers
Seasons: The Complete Seasons of Betrayal Series

Gun Moll Trilogy

Gun Moll
Gangster Moll
Madame Moll

The Chicago War

Deathless & Divided
Reckless & Ruined
Scarless & Sacred
Breathless & Bloodstained
The Complete Series
Maldives & Mistletoe

The Russian Guns

The Arrangement
The Life
The Score
Demyan & Ana
Shattered
The Jersey Vignettes

FANTASY ROMANCE

The Hunted: A 9INE REALMS Novel

Find more on Bethany-Kris's website at www.bethanykris.com.

www.ingramcontent.com/pod-product-compliance
Lightning Source LLC
Chambersburg PA
CBHW071438260626
47170CB00008B/2767